THE ANGLER'S TALE

JACK BENTON

"The Angler's Tale"
Copyright © Jack Benton / Chris Ward 2020

The right of Jack Benton / Chris Ward to be identified as the Author of this Work has been asserted by him in accordance with the Copyright, Designs and Patents Act 1988.

All rights reserved. No part of this publication may be reproduced, stored in a retrieval system, or transmitted, in any form or by any means without the prior written permission of the Author.

This story is a work of fiction and is a product of the Author's imagination. All resemblances to actual locations or to persons living or dead are entirely coincidental.

*For the real Alan McDonald,
the finest of men*

THE ANGLER'S TALE

1

John Hardy pulled the REDUCED sticker off the little cardboard box and peered through the plastic lid at the iced sponge cake inside. He smiled. Small enough not to threaten his nickname of "Slim", but large enough for a celebration.

He dropped it into his basket, as an afterthought adding a pack of candles.

A gong sounded from somewhere overhead. Slim glanced at his watch: 3 a.m. Only the dead and the solitary shopped at such a time, and since he felt more or less alive he had to fall into the other category.

Giving the closed booze aisle a wide berth, he headed for the home goods aisle.

Might as well add a token present.

He paused, rubbing the stubble on his chin as he peered at the gloomy shelves, the overhead lights on half-power here. Perhaps a roll of duct tape to hold down the curling corner of living room carpet, or a new mop and bucket to fight the mould creeping across the kitchen floor.

Camping gear appealed, the idea of vanishing into the wilderness, never to return, but his budget was fifteen quid and the cheapest tents were over twenty.

He settled on a beginner fishing set, £14.99.

Perfect.

He had once briefly lived on a canal, but the closest he had come to fishing was begging outside the local chip shop for a few leftovers at closing time. How hard could it be? The set even came with a small instruction booklet in plastic wrap rolled around the thickest section of rod.

With a smile that for once felt genuine rather than ironic, he picked up the set and balanced it across the top of his basket.

He ate his cake when he got home half an hour later, wished himself happy birthday, and washed it down with a coffee thick and bitter enough to wake the dead.

Then, conversely, he lay on his bed and tried to sleep, staring at the ceiling for a pointless hour before rising again, taking a shower and then brewing another coffee.

He had some stale bread so he toasted it as black as his coffee then doused it in butter and crunched it while he stared at a local Ordnance Survey map.

There. The River Tewkes, leading into Longwell Reservoir. Far enough away from any real civilisation that he could enjoy his birthday in peace.

It was just getting light outside so Slim headed out. He bought a wrapped sandwich and a bottle of water from a corner shop, then located a bus stop with a line that stopped within walking distance of the river. An hour later he was trudging along a narrow, overgrown lane that meandered its way down into a river valley. The Tewkes, twenty feet wide in places, flowed languidly through pastureland. Finding a dry, grassy spot hidden from the field by a stand of trees, Slim laid down a blanket and set up his gear.

It was a quarter past ten when he poked the hook through a piece of ham taken from his sandwich and made his first cast. It struck the water's surface with a comforting plop and sank out of sight. Slim watched the little float bobbing up and down, feeling a rare sense of calm. He smiled at the ease of it all, wondering if catching an actual fish was even necessary. With the line extending out into the water and the rod propped up on a rock, he lay back on his blanket and closed his eyes.

2

THE MISSED CALL WAS FROM KIM, HIS ELDERLY SECRETARY.

'I wondered if you'd be coming into the office tomorrow,' she said when he made the call back that evening.

'Actually, I was thinking of taking a short holiday,' Slim said.

'Well, you're the boss after all. I can keep things going while you're away. However, I will need to forward a few messages which require your response, if that's at all possible. I know you're picky about your cases, but you're turning down a lot of good work being so finicky about what you take on. Have you ever thought about hiring more staff?'

Slim shook his head. With his phone held against his ear with one hand, he opened a birthday card with the other, pushing his nails under the seam and splitting it along the gum line.

The light scent of a familiar perfume revealed the sender before he opened it. Lia. Slim stared at the name for a long time, then ran a finger over the line added at the bottom.

Call me sometime.

He would. Perhaps.

'…I mean, many of these cases are routine,' Kim was saying, although Slim had filtered out a large portion of her discourse as he remembered the few blissful days with Lia before he had broken his sobriety at a family party and things had gone wrong again. 'You could have someone doing the basic investigations and the drudge work while you concentrate on more intricate things.'

'I hear what you're saying, Kim.'

'I'm not sure you do, Mr. Hardy. I know it's not my place to tell you how to run your business, but with the press you've received over the last couple of years, you could be running a six-figure business by now. I've seen your accounts … and you can barely afford to pay me. I don't know how you get by on what little's left. I've had to buy toilet roll out of the petty cash because the fee from the Webster fraud case won't be deposited until next week.'

'We have petty cash?'

'It's that jar under your desk that you always raid for your coffee.'

'It's empty.'

'I know it is. I started putting the money somewhere else because it was disappearing quicker than I could top it up.'

Slim couldn't help but smile. Kim was like the mother his own had never been. He rarely thought about the woman who had brought him into the world, but when he did it was of snoring behind a closed door as he left for school, or fake fur wrapped so tight it could have choked her as she headed out, leaving meals uncooked, rooms uncleaned, an ashtray full on the kitchen table, sometimes an empty bottle or two, and the sensation that his presence in her life was an unwanted one, an unnecessary burden.

At his mother's funeral he had promised he would never end up like her, but in many ways he was a mirror image.

'Thanks for thinking about me,' he said. 'I'll keep it in mind. By the way, do you know how to cook a fish?'

'What kind of fish?'

Slim glanced across at the kitchen tabletop. The single fish he had caught lay on a chopping board with a knife beside it, awaiting its destiny.

'It's about eight inches long. I caught it in a river.'

'Could be trout. Top and tail it, gut it and put it under the grill, a minute or two on each side.'

'Can't it be deep fried? I was thinking of grabbing a portion of chips, make a real celebration of it.'

'Celebration?'

'My birthday.'

'Oh, well, I mean, I must have seen it on your documents somewhere—'

Slim smiled. 'It's okay. I'm not one for parties or anything like that.'

Kim sighed. 'Well, it's probably not a good idea to deep fry it unless you know what you're doing, and men usually don't. If you're not careful you could burn your house down.'

'I'm on the top floor of three,' he said. 'The two below would be safe, wouldn't they?'

From the other end of the line came a long groan. 'Sometimes, Mr. Hardy, I think you need a good woman at home to keep you in order.'

Slim couldn't help but smile. 'Are you offering?'

'That depends on the pension plan. I'm not sure I have the legs in me to keep picking up after you. It's hard enough keeping your office tidy. So, where are you off to?'

'I'm going on a fishing holiday,' Slim said. 'Along the Dart Estuary. I'll be back by the end of the week.'

He hadn't booked it yet, but as he said the words he ran his finger along the catalogue he had picked up in the free rack in the local newsagent, his finger hovering over the phone number.

'It sounds nice, Mr. Hardy. I suppose you have to do what you have to do, in order to escape the trappings of fame.'

'I'm sure I'll be hounded mercilessly,' he said. 'I'm thinking of buying a new jacket to confuse them.'

'You'd better consider something other than grey-green or black in that case,' Kim said. 'You are, of course, aware of the existence of other colours?' She started chuckling at her own joke, before adding, 'In all seriousness, I wish you a good trip.'

'Thanks.'

For a few minutes they talked over what business Kim could handle without help while he was away, and for what he would need to be contactable. He had hoped to disappear, but was finding that the arms of the world refused to let him go now that he had a business which, despite his best efforts at self-sabotage, was proving a moderate success.

Perhaps Kim was right. Perhaps he should employ

someone to run things in his name, allowing him to slip quietly away into whatever sense of oblivion he chose.

But that would be the easy option.

A fishing trip for people trying to stay off the booze. Rehab in all but name.

He had left that part out of their conversation.

He dialled the number and found his hands shaking as he waited for someone to answer.

'How may I help you?' came a pleasant woman's voice.

'Uh ... hello. I'd like to ask about availability for next week.'

There was a short pause. Slim considered hanging up. Then, the same woman's voice said, 'We have a number of vacancies on several of our tours. Did you have any particular location in mind?'

3

Dartmouth's Castle View Hotel lived up to its name only by a sliver if one craned one's neck from the outer corner of the front terrace to see past the edge of the neighbouring property's high garden walls, but nevertheless the view of Kingswear on the opposite hill across the Dart Estuary was as impressive as anything Slim had ever seen. To the south, the hills opened up to reveal the English Channel beyond the river's mouth, while to the north, the river swung languidly up through imposing forested hills spotted with luxury homes, the masts of dozens of moored yachts glittering in the sun like shiny needles.

Set on a steep hillside, by the time Slim had climbed the thirty-five steps from the road up to the hotel's entrance, he was too tired to explore the terraced gardens accessed through a gate to the rear. A narrow front patio was home to several benches, picnic tables, and sun loungers, so Slim got a coffee from the self-service machine inside the dining room and took it outside.

A few other guests were enjoying the afternoon sunshine, some talking, others sipping coffee or fruit juice, one man crunching an oat bar which sent a cascade of crumbs over his knees with each bite. Slim took a seat at an empty table and gazed out across the valley, idly watching a couple of sightseeing ferries pass each other, one heading directly across to Kingswear, the other upriver in the direction of Totnes. A short distance north on the far bank, a party of canoeists explored the inlets beneath the trees, while on the near side a tourist-laden paddle steamer worked its way between two moored yachts, both large and spectacular enough to be worth more than the hotel rising over Slim's shoulder.

'Makes you want to quit your job and move down, doesn't it?' came a voice from behind him. As a shadow fell over Slim, the man added, 'What's your line of work?'

Slim paused before answering, hunting a suitably passive answer that would satisfy this yet unseen stranger without provoking further questions.

'I'm in research,' he said at last, realising as the words came out that he'd chosen the worst possible thing to say.

'What kind?' the newcomer said, pulling a plastic chair out from beneath an adjacent table and setting it down across from Slim. 'Consumer? No, I bet it's educational. I thought so. You have the look of a man fighting injustice. There's a story in your eyes, I can see it.'

Slim wasn't sure how to respond. He regarded the newcomer for a few seconds, taking in a face in its early sixties, a deeply unfashionable moustache spoiling weathered but otherwise handsome features. Eyes that wanted to know more than was due darted about, examining Slim's appearance but at the same time taking in the other guests sitting across the patio, sizing them up, judging them one by one.

'I'm sure you're wondering what I'm doing here,' the man said. 'I mean, you would, wouldn't you?' He reached up and tugged his mustache. 'The disguise ... it's not a great effort, is it?'

Slim forced a smile. 'Do I know you from somewhere?'

The man flashed a sideways grin and nodded furtively as though this were the expected response. He stuck out a hand.

'Max Carson. It's my voice, not my face that you remember. I host Country Club?'

'Right.'

'Radio Three. Are you a regular listener?'

Slim, who didn't own a radio and had rarely had cause to listen to one since his military days ended, said, 'Things got on top of you, too?'

Carson nodded. 'It was my wife who insisted. She couldn't handle the affairs, the booze and the Charles.'

Slim frowned. 'Charles?'

Carson grimaced. 'I'm being deliberately cryptic. You never know who's listening, do you? Every man and his goddamn dog carries a hidden camera these days.' He shifted closer, glanced over his shoulder, then pulled something out of a bag at his feet. Slim glimpsed a whisky miniature hidden inside Carson's big hand as it visited his mouth with a quick jerk and then dropped out of sight again.

Slim had a moment of realisation. He had been thinking about more mundane things, but now it made sense. Charles. Charlie. Cocaine. Max Carson was a man from a fast lane Slim's broken-down car of a life had never known.

'Anyway,' Carson continued, slipping the miniature back into his bag before Slim could get any ideas about asking for a turn, 'you have to go through the motions, sometimes, don't you? It's easier to keep things out of sight and out of mind when you're out of the public eye, isn't it? I bet no one's peering over your shoulder to see who you're sleeping with?'

Slim, whose rocky patch with Lia had now lasted longer than their briefly euphoric good patch, just shrugged. 'Not that I know of,' he said. 'No one much cares what I do in my private life.'

'That's the thing, isn't it?' Carson said, making himself comfortable. 'I don't doubt she has lovers of her own. I mean, I've caught her whistling while she's making up the beds. It wouldn't surprise me if half of Manchester has been through my bedroom while I've been out on location, but I have one little fling, do one little gram ... and my career's on the line. Ridiculous, isn't it?'

'Quite,' Slim agreed.

Carson took him by the shoulder and leaned close. 'I'm sensing we're cut from the same cloth, you and me. Didn't come down here for the fishing, did you? Not the kind on the brochure, at any rate.' He pushed Slim's shoulder until Slim had no choice but to turn in the direction of two middle-aged ladies sitting a couple of tables to their right. Both were a little overdressed, and while Slim saw only two faded wallflowers touched up just enough to turn the occasional reminiscent eye, he remembered Carson had nearly two decades on him. 'I bet neither did they.'

'I suppose you'd have to ask them,' Slim said.

Carson grinned as one looked up and threw him a quick smile before ducking her head away. Cheeks painted with blusher appeared to take on an additional tint, although Slim supposed it could have been a reflection of the tabletop lacquer. 'I already did. What's say you and I head down to the harbour this evening and pick out a boat for a little river cruise? I could do with a wingman.'

Slim felt an urge to wash. He eased Carson's hand off his shoulder and stood up. 'While I appreciate the offer, I'm afraid I already have an appointment for tonight,' he said, flashing a smile. 'With my room and a newspaper.'

Carson's countenance darkened. 'Well, don't come back begging me for another try tomorrow,' he said. 'Nobodies like you don't get second chances with somebodies like me. I'm telling you, there are women in this town with more money than brains, and who cares about a husband off on his yacht somewhere?'

Slim resisted the urge to punch Carson in the face.

'It was nice to meet you, Mr. Carson,' he said. 'If I spot a clean beer mat lying around I'll come and find you for an autograph.'

As Slim made his way back into the hotel, he heard a coarse, 'Don't bother!' aimed at his back, and wondered quite how low his karma stocks had fallen for him to have made an enemy on his first evening.

4

That night there was an arranged social event in the hotel's banquet room. A trestle table laden with party food stood along one wall, with other tables and chairs haphazardly arranged around a politely sized dance floor. After an initial introduction and welcome speech by one of the tour company's representatives, the guests were left to mingle. Slim, frustrated that there was a jug of orange juice and another of dandelion and burdock of all things, but no hot coffee, lingered near a window with a view out over the river.

Max Carson was nowhere to be seen, much to Slim's relief. There was also no sign of either of the women Carson had been eyeing up, suggesting that there had been some truth to the aging radio personality's claims. That or they were fighting a different kind of addiction and had realised a walk down through the village would be of more interest than the welcome event. Slim, feeling more and more like sneaking out to the nearest pub and to hell with recovery, was envious.

Worried he was beginning to look conspicuous, Slim reached into his back pocket and withdrew the folded tour brochure he had been handed on arrival. Another folded piece of card came out with it, and Slim stared at the crumpled remains of the birthday card Lia had sent him. He closed his eyes, thinking of calling her, then shook his head. No. It was better to let her go. She was fifteen years his junior, in the prime of her life. She didn't need to ruin what should be her best years while he limped and struggled along beside her. It didn't matter that she wanted to. It didn't matter that she said that she loved him.

Sometimes, he thought, it was possible to disguise love with sympathy, and the misplacement of either could cause more hurt than it could remove.

A wastepaper basket poked out from beneath the nearest table. He went to throw the card away but changed his mind, sliding it back into his rear pocket. He would likely forget it when he next did his laundry anyway.

The tour brochure offered five days of combined fishing and sightseeing trips, coupled with evening social events. Everything was designed to be low stress and companionable, casually drawing the guests away from what life perils had jogged them into signing up. He had already overheard two men sharing gambling ills, one who had lost his family and another hanging on to his by a thread. Nearby, a pair of middle-aged women barely held back tears as they talked, one lamenting a sex addiction which had broken up her marriage and forced her husband into suicide, the other fighting depression and PTSD after a car accident in which the taking of too many prescription painkillers had resulted in her nodding off at the wheel and hitting a truck head on, killing her young son and his school friend who had been larking about, unbelted, in the back.

Suddenly a little alcoholism seemed like nothing. Slim picked at some finger food for a few minutes then went out to the lobby, where to his great relief the self-service drinks machine was still switched on. He grabbed a coffee then headed for the outdoor patio.

With a firm, chilly wind blowing in off the river, the patio was empty. Slim sat and watched the lights of the town below glittering off the water. A couple of boats moved among the static lights of the dozens of moored yachts, perhaps late night fishermen or pleasure seekers taking some alone time away from the tourist crowds. At the thought of couples enjoying each others' company, Slim pulled his phone from his pocket and opened up the messages, thinking of sending one to Lia.

As he stared at the blinking icon, however, he knew he had nothing meaningful to say. *I'm sorry.* What for? *Me being me. For being as useless as I told you I would be, for letting you down as I said I would, for dragging you into my tempest and letting the storm of my life rag you and toss you aside. I'm sorry for everything I told you would happen.*

With a frown, he switched off his phone and put it away, then took a sip of coffee that wasn't nearly strong enough.

He didn't sleep particularly well, but a few hours were

better than none at all. The room's phone woke him, an automated service calling him down to breakfast.

The bleary eyes around him made it clear some of the other guests had already fallen prey to their personal demons. Max Carson was again nowhere to be seen; he had no doubt been lucky or unlucky, depending on the circumstances. Slim sat at a table for four. On one side was an overweight lady with a scrunched face who introduced herself with a smoker's rasp as Irene Long. On his other was a young girl with long hair and wide, unblinking eyes. Eloise Trebuchet. Opposite sat a big man with a thick beard running up to eyes shaded by an overhanging brow. He didn't introduce himself nor even glance in Slim's direction, but a self-written name tag pinned to his shirt pocket labelled him as George Slade.

Before Slim could attempt a conversation, a tour rep stood up and called for quiet. The man, around thirty, handsome and smart in a blue shirt and checkered tie, introduced himself in an overtly flustered manner as Alex Wade. A colleague standing off to the side was Jane Hounslow. Alex continued, talking through the day's itinerary while wiping sweat off his brow, leaving his sleeve visibly damp.

An hour later, Slim found himself sitting in the prow of a motorboat with a chill river breeze ruffling his hair. Eight other people sat around him, including Irene from breakfast. The group had been split into three, with his breakfast companions George Slade and Eloise Trebuchet allocated to one of the other two boats. As they bumped and skidded over the choppy water's surface, Alex pointed out various local sights, but otherwise there was little conversation.

The first stop was a small inlet a couple of miles upriver where they disembarked at a rickety pier and followed a narrow path leading beneath the trees to a spot where Alex claimed they would find good perch and carp in beneath the riverbank. It was clear from the tackle carried by the passengers that the group ran the gauntlet from wannabe pros to complete beginners. While some had their own gear, others borrowed rods and tackle from the boat before making their way to secluded spots along the riverbank where deckchairs had already been arranged in the shade beneath the trees. There, they were left to their thoughts, with the guide, Alex, stopping past every thirty minutes or so.

Slim, proud to have remembered all his tackle, nevertheless caught only a piece of passing driftwood which became tangled in the line. A couple of fish had disturbed the water's surface nearby, however, and he was convinced he was heading for a major catch when Alex wandered past and informed him it was time to move on.

What followed was lunch on the boat and then a trip to a local sightseeing spot where the group climbed a steep path through the forest up to the ruins of a stone-age hilltop fort. Despite a few grumbles, most people seemed in good spirits, and Slim found himself sharing pleasantries about the view with a Londoner called Dan who mentioned something offhand about a recently completed prison sentence.

After a short lecture on the site's history, the group were given twenty minutes to wander before heading back down to the pier. Upon reaching it, they found an agitated Alex talking on his mobile phone, and as the guests climbed back into the boat, Alex's look of dismay grew. When everyone was assembled, he ended his call then signalled to the driver to wait before starting the engine.

'Can I have everyone's attention, please? I'm afraid we have to cut short the day's excursion.' He paused to wipe his brow before taking a deep breath. 'There's been an incident.'

5

Alex refused to give any specific answers until everyone was back in the hotel's banquet and function room, insisting that he knew little more than they the reason for the group's unexpected recall. All sorts of rumours were circulating, but when two police officers climbed onto a podium at the far end of the room, Slim knew it was serious.

With everyone assembled, Alex took a microphone and called for order. As the hush settled, he introduced the police officers as PC Dave Rogers and WPC Marion Oaks. WPC Oaks, a slim, pretty lady a full head taller than her squat, muscular counterpart, took the microphone and cleared her throat.

'I apologise for interrupting your day's activities,' she said. 'I'll get straight to the point. There's been an accident.'

A ripple of noise passed through the crowd. Slim, standing near the back, glanced at Irene standing nearby. She had a hand over her mouth, her eyes already tearful.

'Early this morning the body of a Mr. Max Carson, a guest on your tour, was found near Greenway House, a couple of miles upriver. Greenway House, as you may be aware, is owned by the National Trust and is a famous local tourist attraction. Mr. Carson is believed to have fallen from an unfinished railway bridge on an abandoned section of the Kingswear-to-Paignton line, a fall of approximately thirty feet. Early coroner's reports suggest he died from a broken neck.'

As questions rose out of the ensuing noise, WPC Oaks lifted a hand. 'There's not a lot more I can tell you at this stage,' she said. 'Our investigation is still in progress. However, I would like to ask that all of you remain here at the hotel for the next forty-eight hours, until we have spoken with each of you. If anyone has what you believe to be relevant information, please come forward in a few minutes and get the attention of PC Rogers or myself. I'd like to mention that none of you is considered implicit in anything that might have occurred. We simply wish to establish Mr. Carson's last movements, and whether anything he said gave a clue as to what later transpired.'

Regardless of the police officer's words, people began to mutter among themselves about the falling eyes of suspicion, about how someone in the room had to be guilty of something. With so many fragile people present, within a couple of minutes several had begun to cry, one wailing so loudly that a couple of hotel staff helped the sobbing figure from the room.

Slim slipped into observation mode, finding a place near the wall from where to watch proceedings. Alex and Jane had taken up positions at the back of the room from where they were dispensing information about the likely course of events. Slim caught snippets of conversion about refunds, reschedules, upsets caused to recoveries, and various veiled accusations that the incident was in some way the tour operator's fault.

'Why do you think he offed himself?'

Slim jumped at the sound of the voice at his shoulder. Eloise stood there, her intense gaze fixed on the two police officers answering queries from the stage. One hand brushed a curtain of hair away from her face, tucking it behind her ear.

'Excuse me?'

The girl shifted from foot to foot as though she was late on a medicinal dose. A smile, unsure of its welcome, came and went like a nervous twitch. 'I mean, he must have, otherwise they'd be a little more careful about keeping us from mixing, in case we were getting our stories straight.'

'You're familiar with police procedures?' Slim asked.

'Got into training college once,' Eloise said, still not looking at him. 'First case as a trainee I borrowed a bag of drugs from a haul and got myself a habit. Things went downhill from there.'

Her expression settled into a wide grin as she continued to stare straight ahead. It was hard to tell whether she was telling the truth, and the absence of any emotion in her eyes made Slim shiver.

'I suppose they would,' he said at last, wishing he were up in his room.

'You know the bastard propositioned me last night?' Eloise said. 'Told me he knew what would make me cook and offered to throw in a couple of hundred to make the deal into a steal.' She was still smiling as she spoke but now her smile dropped. 'His exact words. I told him it wouldn't be a good idea to indulge while I was still on probation.' Finally she looked at him, her eyes blazing. 'I stabbed a guy who tried to rape me.'

Wishing she would look away, he said, 'The guy probably deserved it.'

Eloise shrugged. 'He did. I got first degree murder reduced to self-defence, but because I let him bleed out instead of calling for help, I got five years. The judge suggested I was callous. He was right. I wanted the bastard to die slower than he did, and I was prepared to sit there all night.'

Eloise didn't look old enough to have spent five years in prison, but Slim had learned the hard way that looks could be deceiving. Not trusting his tongue, he said nothing, but remembered a time he had tried to kill a man with a razor blade for sleeping with his now-ex-wife.

'Believe it or not, I can sympathise,' he said. 'I'm no angel myself.'

'Why are you here?'

'I drink too much,' he said, aware how casual it sounded after her confession.

'How much?'

Slim grimaced. 'Enough to lose my mind from time to time.'

'Do you black out?'

Slim shrugged. 'Sometimes. It's been a while, though. I've been fairly ... restrained of late.'

Eloise's eyes flickered across his face as though trying to memorise the pieces of a puzzle. 'I doubt you'll fall under too much suspicion then,' she said. 'I'm expecting to be cuffed at any moment. Luckily I have an alibi.' That insane grin again. 'I was in bed with Alex.'

'The rep?' Slim remembered how flustered their guide had appeared at the morning meeting.

'Another cat among pigeons, as I'm sure screwing the customers is against company policy,' she said. 'I imagine he didn't expect the last few hours of his job to be so dramatic.' She gave half a shrug. 'I'm sure he'll deny it, but I can prove it, if you know what I mean. Kind of a personal policy.' She grinned. 'A safety net.'

Slim had a nagging urge to end the conversation. Just by being in Eloise's presence he felt a taint of her obvious insanity trickling into him.

'Here they come,' Eloise said, as PC Rogers got down off the stage and made his way through the crowd in their direction. Eloise, as though readying herself to unleash a prepared speech, smiled, briefly closing her eyes. As the last group in front of them parted, however, it was Slim to whom the police officer turned.

'Mr. John Hardy?'

'Yes?'

'Do you mind if we have a word? We'd like to establish your movements during the afternoon and evening of yesterday. It appears you were the last person we can verify to having seen Mr. Carson alive.'

6

A SMALL MEETING ROOM AT THE HOTEL'S REAR WAS FAR nicer than an interrogation cell might have been. Slim sat on a plain office chair, facing the two police officers.

'I'd like to point out that you're not under suspicion of anything,' PC Rogers told him, legs crossed as he leaned back in a plush leather chair most likely reserved for the head of a board meeting. 'We just need to establish what contact you had with Max Carson.'

Slim sipped a coffee they had offered him before clearing his throat. 'I spoke to him last night, shortly after arriving. I found him, for want of a better description, to be a clown of the highest degree. I'm happy to detail what I remember of our conversation but I don't know if it will help.'

'It might,' PC Rogers said. 'It could provide a clue as to his frame of mind.'

'He wanted me to play wingman while he pursued a couple of women whom he considered available. I refused his offer and we parted on poor terms.'

PC Rogers jotted something down on a notepad. 'Could you identify these women?'

'If you showed me a picture I'm sure I could. They were sitting right behind us on the patio. I didn't see them there today, although perhaps they were part of a different group.'

The two police officers exchanged a glance. 'We'll see what we can arrange,' WPC Oaks said. 'What's your line of work, Mr. Hardy?'

'I'm a private detective.'

WPC Oaks patted PC Rogers' arm. 'I thought so. Slim Hardy, aren't you? You busted—'

Slim lifted a hand. 'I'm no celebrity,' he said. 'I came here to try my hand at fishing for a week.'

'On a rehab trip for recovering addicts?'

'I have a problem with the bottle,' Slim said. 'Most of the time I'm functioning, but not often enough. In my line of work I need a crutch to fall back on once in a while. I'm sure you understand.'

The police officers exchanged another glance. Slim leaned forward. 'I'm not at liberty to ask, but I'm more used to asking questions than answering them. Carson topped himself, didn't he? You're just trying to make sure it wasn't staged.'

PC Rogers uncrossed his legs and leaned forward. 'Our investigation is ongoing, Mr. Hardy,' he said. 'I can't officially comment on the case until it's either concluded or a public statement is made by police. Unofficially, however, that's exactly what happened. Last night he went out to Greenway House, famous as I'm sure you know, as the summer residence of one late Agatha Christie. What's less well known is that in the lower grounds of the gardens is a disused railway cutting which ends in the collapsed remains of an unfinished steel bridge. Sometime around five or six a.m., according to the coroner's report, Carson threw himself off. It didn't take much to uncover that Carson was a man with debts, a drug problem, and a contract unlikely to be renewed once his wife made public details of numerous affairs in a tabloid story due to run this coming Sunday. Carson, by every intent and purpose, had plenty of reasons to be up on that bridge.'

Another glance passed between the two police officers, as though silently considering whether to let Slim in on their secret.

'However,' PC Rogers began, 'the question we have is why he was tied up.'

'His hands were tied?'

WPC Oaks shook her head. 'Not his hands, Mr. Hardy. His feet.'

7

Slim was relieved of the urge to call Lia by voluntarily relinquishing his phone for twenty-four hours until initial interviews with all the guests had been concluded. He headed back to his room, where he sat at a desk and tried to read a complimentary newspaper. His thoughts, however, strayed continuously to the case of the dead radio DJ and the few details the police had been willing to share.

Carson had fallen to his death, but not before appearing to tie his own feet together. The initial coroner's report suggested that particles found on Carson's hands as well as the angle of rope burns on his ankles confirmed he had tied his feet himself before falling—backwards, claimed the report—off the end of the path to the tangle of metal half buried in the reeds below.

There was more, Slim was certain, but he didn't blame the police for not sharing. Were he in their position, he would no more trust a private investigator than he would a prime suspect. However, the openness of their questioning suggested it was a clear case of suicide, with a couple of irregularities complicating matters. Carson, in retrospect, had come across as a deeply unhappy but proud man. Aware his pedestal was about to topple, he might have tried to go out with a bang.

There was no curfew keeping him in his room, so after a few minutes of quiet contemplation, Slim headed back downstairs. A table had been set up for drinks and snacks, while Alex and Jane were loitering in the lobby, ready to answer any questions. Slim spotted Irene, deep in conversation with Jane, her chubby face wet with tears. Slim caught a furtive 'this trip was my last chance' as he moved past to get a coffee.

He was standing on his own, looking out of a window at the lights glittering along the River Dart estuary when Alex sheepishly tapped him on the shoulder.

'Mr. Hardy,' he said. 'I've not yet had an opportunity to apologise for the unfortunate events of this morning and the disruption it's caused to your trip. We've since spoken to head office and a full refund will be issued.'

'Not to worry,' Slim said. 'It was going on work expenses anyway. I planned to use it as a tax break.' At Alex's confused look, he added, 'That was a joke.'

'Well, in any case, I'd like to apologise again.'

'Does this kind of thing happen often?' Slim asked. 'I mean, you're dealing with a high risk group of individuals.'

Alex looked uncertain about how much information he ought to divulge. 'We've had breakdowns, of course,' he said. 'Lots of people quit and leave early. This isn't rehab, more recovery. We have no strict protocols. However, this is our first suicide.'

'If indeed it was one,' Slim said.

'What makes you think it wasn't?'

Slim shrugged. Unsure whether it was wise to stir the pot, he said, 'Carson seemed in good spirits when I spoke to him.'

'Were you acquainted?'

'Not at all. We just exchanged pleasantries.' Unable to resist, he added, 'I knew him by reputation, of course. The tabloid one.'

'We've hosted a few people in similar situations,' Alex said. 'You've had a few column inches of your own.'

'None were deserved,' Slim said. 'In any case, thanks for keeping me up to date. I would like to continue the tour if that's an option.'

Alex looked surprised. 'Well, of course it is. We might have a few holdups for the next couple of days but I'm assured that within forty-eight hours we'll be free to continue. I'm just surprised you'd want to stay after what's happened.'

The words had come out of Slim's mouth without thought, a knee-jerk reaction rather than something he had really considered. However, the uncertainties around Carson's suicide had piqued his interest. Like a man unable to drive past a car crash without pulling over to watch the bodies being cut from the wreckage, Slim found himself aching to know what had sent Carson plummeting to his death with his feet tied.

8

SLIM HAD ALWAYS FOUND BOOKS HARD TO GET INTO, BUT with little else to do he procured a couple of battered reference books on the art of fishing and found them remarkably easy to enjoy. He hadn't realised there was so much more to the sport than spearing a worm onto a hook and tossing the line out into the water. While most of the technical jargon was beyond his comprehension, he enjoyed the descriptions of the varieties of fish, and tips on snaring the particular one you were after, as well as the guides to many of the UK's best rivers and lakes.

Early that morning, Alex had knocked on Slim's door. The police wanted to speak to him again. Slim's nerves had jangled, but they had only wanted to inform him that his assistance in the inquiry was no longer required. They returned his phone and said he was free to leave should he wish. He found Alex in the hotel lobby, where he was told an impromptu tour of Dartmouth had been hastily arranged for those guests willing to stay on. With nothing better to do, Slim joined a group outside which included both Irene and Eloise, the younger girl hanging off the older woman's arm as though adopting a surrogate mother. Not wishing to engage in rumour, Slim nevertheless found himself overhearing several conversations about whether the absent guests had simply left or been detained by the police. As they trailed Alex past ornate churches and affluent piers, up and down narrow streets and alleys sometimes so steep they were literally staircases, no one mentioned the details of Carson's death, leaving Slim to presume the shared knowledge had been for him alone.

The tour took them south along the aptly named Above Town Road before jagging downhill to Bayard Cove and back along the waterfront, with Alex providing a running commentary about the famous people who lived in the area, local customs, and historical facts. All of it had a clipped blandness to it as though Alex had memorised the summary page of a local tourism website. By the time the group stopped for lunch in a harbourside fish restaurant, several people were muttering about breaking off from the group and exploring the quaint streets around the harbour by themselves. Slim found himself sitting on the edge of a group discussing the hiring of a water taxi for a trip downriver to Dartmouth Castle.

Alex must have smelled a whiff of mutiny, for as soon as the fidgeting began to intensify, he stood up and announced that the tour was officially over. People quickly dispersed, Eloise blowing a kiss over her shoulder to a grimacing Alex as she hurried to catch up with Irene.

Finding himself alone but with a coffee to finish, Slim

took out his ancient Nokia and checked his messages. Kim had called, leaving a voicemail checking on his availability for a fraud case next week. Slim sent a quick response to say he'd return her call in a couple of days, putting off making a decision. He checked his messages again, as though to make sure none had slipped past the primitive notification sequence, but there was nothing from Lia.

She wouldn't beg. She had calmly said her piece and left it there. It was Slim who had fallen off the rails, lost his way home, got beaten up by thugs in alleyways, who ranted at the only person in the last twenty years who had wanted to spend time with him for no reason other than just because. Even now, weeks after they had parted, some of the things he had said still haunted him. He had pressed the self-destruct button on their relationship and then dared to blame her for giving him a chance.

He stood up. The pub was too close. If he stayed here much longer his brooding would drag him inside. Instead, he headed up the harbourside, trying to find interest in the workings of the river alongside him.

Still early in the summer season, away from the tourist ferry piers outside the Royal Avenue Gardens there were few people. A scattering of deckhands stood winding coils of rope or polishing the railings around small motorboats. At the end of the main pier, past a large park where parents led young children in games of football and cricket, Slim found a boatyard where one small vessel had been lifted into the air by a pulley, and a man in overalls was scrapping barnacles off the hull with a chisel.

Slim returned the few greetings he received, but

several people let their eyes linger a little too long before they looked away without comment. His old black jeans, sweater with a hole on one elbow, and the wisp of beard he had forgotten to shave for the last couple of days, marked him as out of place among the wealth on display. Afraid of looking like a prowling thief, he walked quickly past until he came to a narrow concrete breakwater lined by small fishing boats. As rust and Wellington boots replaced shiny chrome and expensive London brands, Slim relaxed. A couple of older men with broad shoulders and tatty hats greeted him warmly as they hauled lobster pots out of a boat and dumped them onto the harbourside. Slim watched for a while, then offered a polite, 'Decent catch today?'

The nearest of the men stood up straight and rubbed his back. 'Could always be better,' he said with a genial smile. 'Ain't that the truth of everything?'

Slim nodded. 'No truer words than those.'

'You in the trade, lad?' the other asked. He had a grey-flecked beard and wore a heavy knit sweater. As he propped a waterproofed boot up onto an upturned bucket, Slim smiled and said, 'No, but sometimes I wish I was.'

'There's something to be said for the ocean-going life,' the first man chuckled. 'A shame we rarely go farther than the English Channel.'

'Boat wouldn't hold up,' the second man added. 'Although waters out there can rage like Old Bea when they want. People look at that little strip of sea and think nothing of it, but we've seen many a rough night out there.'

Slim smiled. 'I can imagine.'

The two men gazed out towards the mouth of the Dart Estuary and the English Channel beyond. Out on the horizon, a couple of tankers passed each other, while closer, a small sailboat bounced in the choppy water.

'You're one of those recovery lot, aren't you?' the second man said abruptly, turning and fixing Slim with a stare. 'I should have realised. Used to be these towns were for work, then it was tourism, now it's therapy. I hope whatever you're buggered with is giving you a bit of respite down here.'

'The bottle,' Slim said, figuring if anyone might understand, it would be two battle-hardened fishermen. 'And yeah, I'm feeling better than I have in a while.'

The second man grinned. 'I'm sure we could find you a spot onboard if you were looking,' he said. 'Drink as much as you like then throw it up in the chop on the way out each morning. Got some shoulders about you. Work in haulage?'

'I used to be a soldier. First Gulf War.'

The first man gave a respectful nod. Slim's sole active tour of duty was the one thing about him able to draw such a response. 'Probably averse to a bit of sand in that case,' the sailor said. 'Don't worry, lad, we work off piers. Here some days, Torquay on others, sometimes down as far as Fowey. The Gulf War, eh? I imagine that explains the bottle.'

Slim nodded. 'Some.'

'Must have been a shock what happened with that old guy,' the second said.

'Heard he had a name,' the first said. 'Radio or something.'

'Max Carson,' Slim said. 'The police said it was suicide.'

The two fishermen exchanged a glance. 'They would,' the first said, as the second nodded. 'Better if it was.'

Slim wanted to ask what they meant, but both men turned their backs to him, resuming their work. He stood still a few seconds longer, feeling the breeze on his face. The men took up their conversation where it had been before his interruption, and from the way their bodies closed against him, it became clear that further questions were no longer welcome.

9

Back near the tourist ferry pier, Slim bought a paper cup of weak, sour coffee from a Spar, then found a bench in the Royal Avenue Gardens with a view across the river to Kingswear. As he watched a couple of yachts passing, he pulled out his Nokia and called Donald Lane, an old platoon mate who had set up an intelligence agency in London after leaving the army.

'Don? It's Slim. How are you doing?'

'Slim! Good to hear from you. It's been a couple of months since we last spoke, and I was starting to wonder what happened to you. How are things?'

'Up and down,' Slim said. 'I'm on a holiday of sorts. I had to take time out of the game before the game took time out of me. It was going all right until someone decided to ruin it by jumping off a railway cutting and killing himself, at least according to the official story. A man named Max Carson, a well-known radio DJ. I wondered if you could have a little dig into his background, just to see what might have pushed him over the edge. Or who.'

'Easy. Consider it done.'

Slim thanked Don and hung up. The sky was clouding over, the crystal blue replaced by an unfolding blanket of moody grey. Slim headed back towards the hotel, hoping to get a little quiet time on the patio before the groups rolled in for dinner. Bored with the main thoroughfare, though, he cut up through some back streets, and soon found himself sidetracked by a succession of quaint trinket shops.

Not long ago, his only possessions had been the clothes on his back, and while Slim prayed those days were behind him, he still found it hard to throw money at useless ornaments and souvenirs. Instead, as he wandered in and out of narrow doorways propped open by whitewashed chairs and pseudo pirate chests, he thought about what Lia might like for her pretty flat in the Derbyshire Peak District. Even when spending money had been something done without forethought, Slim had always preferred locally made goods, and was soon browsing a gallery devoted to local artists, admiring framed prints of different views of the Dart Estuary. He found one he thought would look nice in Lia's kitchen— or at worst, in a corner of his dingy office—and joined a queue behind an old couple, before thinking better of it and putting the painting back. Feeling a sudden despondence which in worse times would have reeled him in to the nearest bottle, he turned for the door.

As he did so, he caught sight of a painting propped up behind the clerk's counter, a plastic bag stretched over its top edge as though it were bound for the rubbish bin. To Slim's untrained eye, it appeared to be oil on canvas, and showed a watery inlet flanked by forested hills on either side. Bridging the inlet from one hill to the other was a small railway bridge. A train was emerging from one side, a plume of steam rising into a clear blue sky.

Slim waited until the other customers had paid and left, then approached the clerk.

'Excuse me,' he said. 'May I take a look at that painting?'

The clerk frowned. 'Well, I took it down for a little reordering ... but, I suppose if you'd like.'

He lifted the painting onto the counter and removed the plastic bag. Up close it was an array of frantic dabs of thick paint, lacking the clarity it abruptly gained from a few steps away, clearly the work of a skilled hand.

'Who painted it?' Slim asked.

The clerk pointed to the signature in the bottom right corner. 'Alan McDonald. He's a well-known local artist and also a keen angler. This is a rare original; mostly we only stock prints. He paints from his boat while fishing out in the estuary. He's the only painter who regularly does because of the chop of the water, so you might see him out there sometime in his little motorboat. It gives his paintings a unique perspective.' Then, pointing to a small water stain in one corner, he added, 'As well as a few touches of authenticity.'

Slim nodded. The painting was eighteen inches high and a couple of feet long, certainly a fine centrepiece for a kitchen or dining room. The light blue of the sky contrasted with the darker blue of the water. Flickers of colour beneath the trees suggested spring flowers, while the dark green gave the impression of recent rain. Only a streak of red along the locomotive's body interrupted the earthy colour scheme, but amidst the greys and blacks of the train it seemed to add balance.

'Is that near here?' Slim said.

The clerk looked momentarily surprised again. 'Ah, yes, it's the old railway bridge across the Wellwater Inlet. It's a couple of miles up the Dart Estuary, near Greenway.'

Slim nodded but didn't answer. The clerk, feeling the need to continue the explanation to fill the vacuum of silence, stammered as he said, 'My boss didn't ... didn't think that ... right now was an appropriate time to have it visibly on sale.'

'Why not?' Slim said, figuring that playing innocent might draw out more information than he would otherwise receive.

'Well,' the clerk said, 'Wellwater is where that man was found. I mean, there's only the remains of a bridge there now, and no trains ever ran on it because it wasn't ever finished, but someone local would recognise it.'

Slim decided it was only fair to put the suffering clerk out of his misery. 'Oh, you mean the radio guy? I overheard some men talking about that in the pub. Suicide, wasn't it? Is this where it was?'

'I'm afraid so,' the clerk said, lowering his head.

'I'll tell you what,' Slim said. 'It's a decent picture regardless of its background. If you like, I'll take it off your hands.' With a clumsy wink he added, 'Although a little bit of a discount would make the decision easier.'

The clerk knocked off £55 but the painting still came

in at a hefty £140. Even though it was a steal for original art of such quality, at one time Slim would have baulked at paying that for a new car. Nevertheless, he paid with the business credit card Kim had made him apply for, certain his clever secretary could fiddle the cost as expenses and save him a bit of tax. With the painting in a protective paper bag and tucked under his arm, he headed out of the shop.

He was pausing to adjust the position of a package that was heavier than it looked when he heard footsteps behind him. He turned, surprised to see Eloise appear out of a narrow alleyway leading up the hillside. She glanced up, saw him, and lifted a hand in greeting.

'Shopping?' she said.

'Just a little souvenir.'

Eloise raised an eyebrow. The way they were manicured into angular lines made her look robotic.

'I never took you for much of an art lover. I have to say, I wasn't convinced by the fishing, either.'

Slim resisted the urge to ask when he had been placed on trial. 'I must be a poor actor,' he said.

Eloise flashed a cold smile as she came closer, then suddenly grabbed Slim's arm and leaned against him.

'I know we're not here to make friends,' she said, 'but if you want to share my table at dinner I wouldn't mind at all. I'd like a chance to figure you out.'

Unsure at what point he'd become Eloise's pet project, he just shrugged. 'I suppose I might see you around later.'

'Good.' Another cold smile, but this one came with a gaze peering off into the distance. Slim stared at her, convinced he was witnessing some kind of personality disorder in action. Then, without another word, Eloise was gone, backing away into a side street before ducking her head, turning, and scurrying off. Slim watched her until she was out of sight, wondering if he should have accepted Alex's offer of a refund and taken an early departure after all.

10

He drank coffee in the lobby until the filter was empty, suffered the effects of it half an hour later in the toilet, then stumbled into the dining room thankful at least that he'd not stumbled farther down the road to the nearest pub.

With their party reduced to the bare bones of four small tables, Slim headed for the closest empty chair until he saw Eloise, sitting on the table nearest the far wall, wave him over. An audience with the hollow-eyed girl was the last thing he felt like, but at least Irene Long was also present to dilute the younger girl's intensity.

'I hear you're a bit of an art enthusiast,' Irene said by way of greeting.

'I prefer my souvenirs local,' Slim said. 'I only have a small flat.'

Irene guffawed as though he had told the funniest joke in the world, but Eloise just stared at Slim with the intensity of a cat eyeing up a bird.

'I like art too,' she said. 'I once wanted to be a painter.

I just didn't have the talent.' With a cold smile, she added, 'I might have to visit your room later and take a closer look.'

It came across as a threat rather than an offer of something more. Irene looked away, and Slim smiled as though to pass it off as a joke.

'I wonder what's on tonight's menu,' he said, looking towards the kitchens as a way of breaking Eloise's stare. 'I'd settle for a steak. Of anything.'

He didn't remember anything in the brochure about the restaurant being vegan, but purity in all its forms seemed a gimmick of the tour company. They were free to head into the town as Carson had two nights ago, of course, but in the wake of the old radio DJ's suicide a collective distrust of Dartmouth had settled over the group. With the offer of a full refund, only nine of the original twenty-five had chosen to stay, and those seemed, after dark at least, to take comfort in one another's company.

'Do you think he really topped himself?' Irene said, as bowls of soya gratin arrived. 'I mean, that's what the police said, but they're not going to share details, are they?'

Eloise gave her a typical cold smile. 'If there's more, it'll come out in the next few days,' she said. 'After all, that's why we're all still here, isn't it?'

'That's a very morbid thing to say.'

Eloise shrugged, then looked pointedly at Slim. 'I see no point in wrapping it up in cotton wool. Personally, I think someone here might have been involved.'

'It's not true, though, is it?' Irene said. 'I mean, the police interviewed everyone, and no one got—'

Eloise lifted a hand, rather rudely cutting the older woman off. 'Let's eat. Supposed to be forgetting our troubles, aren't we?'

Slim glanced at Irene, wondering if he ought to speak up, but while Eloise was looking away the older woman just flashed him a pained smile and rolled her eyes. Slim didn't know what had brought Irene here, but if even half of what Eloise had told him about herself was true, he didn't want to get on the younger girl's wrong side.

A glass clinked as Alex stood up. He thanked everyone for staying and then talked through the revised itinerary for the following few days. Tomorrow included a boat trip up to Totnes for some sightseeing in the morning, followed by an introduction to fly fishing in the afternoon.

After half an hour of awkward, stilted conversation, the dinner things were cleared away and the guests began to leave. Without a word, Eloise rose and headed out of the room. Slim glimpsed her taking the stairs up to the guest rooms, so instead followed some others out onto the terrace, where staff distributed soft drinks. A warm breeze drifted in off the Dart, and the view was pretty enough to relieve the stress of the last couple of days. Lights glittered off the river, pleasure boats or late-night fishermen. From down in the town came the distant hum of music out of the local pubs, mixed with the occasional bellow of raucous laughter.

'I know you probably think she's a psychopath, but she's got it into her head that you came down here to knock Carson off,' came a voice from behind him. Slim turned to find Irene standing behind him. She held out a paper cup. 'I'm guessing you like it bitter and black?'

Slim smiled. 'People here seem to know me better than I know myself,' he said. 'Does Eloise really think I'm some kind of assassin?'

'While I'll admit I'm not discounting anything about you, Slim, she does take things to the extreme. Alex told me she's schizophrenic. Delusional, that kind of thing. He said he woke up on the first morning to find her sitting on the edge of his bed, mumbling to herself. When questioned she claimed she had got the wrong room, but since then she's been spreading rumours about them which could get Alex into some trouble. Apparently she had to get a doctor's note to be allowed down here, but that same doctor sent Alex a private message. She has a tendency to forget her medicine.'

'That message didn't stay private for long,' Slim said.

Irene smiled. 'Don't worry, I didn't sleep with him to get it. It's money that runs these people, not our health. If we stay in line they don't care what we do.'

Slim had already been planning to lock his door, but it might be better to just sleep with his bed pushed up against it. He was starting to realise that the demons haunting him were just ants compared to those on the backs of some of the others.

'I'm an alcoholic,' he said, since they appeared to be sharing secrets. 'I have been for as long as can remember. I'm functioning, is how they describe it. I can go long periods without drinking at all, then something will trigger it. I've actually been twelve days sober, my longest in years.'

'Well, good for you.' Irene's smile seemed genuine. 'Todd's Syndrome.'

'What's that? I've not heard of it.'

'I was in a car accident in my early twenties. I thought I had recovered, but ten years later I started to get bouts of strange oppressiveness. I ignored it for a while, but it got worse. I had days when I couldn't open my eyes because everything looked wrong. Chairs were taller than me. Tables were ants at my feet.'

I think I read something about that once.'

'It's more commonly known as Alice in Wonderland Syndrome.' Irene gave a grim smile. 'I think that romanticises it a bit, but there have been times when all I could do was lie curled up in a ball through fear of the world crushing me. I've attempted suicide twice, and my doctor wanted me institutionalised. I refused, and came here looking for a natural cure. As my body adjusts to it, the strength of my medication needs to be increased too often. Soon it'll be at dangerous levels. This really is my last chance.'

Slim could think of nothing to say. He sipped his coffee and watched Irene as she stared out at the glittering Dart Estuary. Eventually, feeling the need to continue the conversation, he said, 'Since I've been here, I've begun to realise that my problems are slight compared to many people. If nothing else, that's been a benefit to me.'

'We can't compare our problems,' Irene said. 'They're all destructive in their own way. I used to lecture on physics at Sheffield University,' she added, causing Slim to raise an eyebrow. She looked nothing like he had ever imagined a scientist would. 'Now I'm mostly unemployable. I got a supermarket job for a while just to get out of the house, but I had to quit after I had a turn at work. I imagine drinking makes it hard to hold down a job, doesn't it?'

Slim nodded. 'That's why I work for myself.'

'Oh? You're self-employed?'

'I'm a private investigator.'

Irene chuckled. 'Poor Eloise would have a field day over that. I thought you looked familiar. Have you ever been on television?'

'Once. Not the most memorable experience I've had, and not one I'm keen to repeat.'

'It must have been a thrill anyway. Out of interest, what's your opinion on all this nasty business with Mr. Carson?'

Slim shrugged. 'I have no reason to disbelieve what the police told me.'

'Is that what you really think? I didn't say much to him, but he didn't seem like the suicide-type. Too pretentious. Me, I think someone was after him.'

Slim laughed it away, but as the words settled into his mind, they found a place to hide there, and took a hold from which he knew it would be difficult to break loose.

11

As usual he slept poorly, and woke with the feeling that Eloise was leaning over him, wearing that psychopathic smile and threatening to cut him open. When he climbed out of bed, however, the room was unchanged from when he went to bed, with no sign that anyone had been inside during the night.

After breakfast, he headed out with the rest of their remaining group, down to the port and onto a pretty motorboat which whisked them up the river to Totnes, where they spent a couple of hours browsing the shops. Slim was mercifully left alone, with Irene and Eloise—who had pointedly ignored him all morning—heading off together. Bored with trinket shopping, Slim wandered around a couple of modern clothing stores, picking up a token pair of socks, before retiring to a café on the high street to sample the brews in this part of south Devon. With little going on outside the window, and only one other customer—an old woman sitting with a Yorkshire terrier nestled at her feet—he toyed with the idea of attempting one of the paperbacks on a rack inside the door. Then his eyes fell on the painting hanging above it, half obscured by a pile of dog-eared airport thrillers.

The signature in the visible bottom right corner was familiar. Alan McDonald. The same painter responsible for the piece wrapped up in Slim's room back at the hotel. This one showed another view of a river inlet. A little fishing boat was moored under a line of overhanging trees, a raft of ducks swimming nearby.

Slim leaned forward, resting his hand on the tabletop below the painting. His fingers came away dusty, but on top of the stack of books to one side, there was none, as though the books had only been placed there in the last day or so.

Carefully he lifted them down to reveal the hidden part of the painting. He frowned, feeling a peculiar chill as he recognised a tumbledown house tucked back among the trees by the water's edge. Standing on a short jetty right outside was a woman, arms folded. It was impossible to make out any features from the painting, except that her legs were pale from the knees down as though she were walking barefoot, and that she was facing and most likely watching the painter as he worked.

Slim put the stack of books back where it had been before. He turned to the café's service counter and caught the server's eye. With a nod, the young man came over.

'You all right there, mate?' the young man asked. 'Anything I can get you? You know, you can borrow any book you like. We're overloaded.'

'I was just looking at that painting,' Slim said. 'I picked up a similar one. I wondered if you knew anything about it?'

The server shrugged. 'Art's not my thing, I'm afraid, mate. You'd have to ask the boss. He's on from three. Not sure if he would know much about it, though. We get local painters bringing stuff around from time to time. They're supposed to be for sale but often they hang there so long the artists just donate them to the shop in the end. Got a couple of the high street out the back if you're interested.'

'No, it's fine,' Slim said. 'I might stop by again later on.'

'Sure, as you like.'

Slim wished the man a good day and headed out. He walked down to the pier where he found the rest of the group waiting to board the boat for the afternoon's activities. Alex gave Slim a frustrated glance as though to suggest he had held them up, then introduced a bearded man in a green rain jacket.

'Terrance Winters,' the man said, holding a long, thin rod up into the air. 'I run Winters' Tackle Shop on Wheelwright Street. Come in any time this week and you'll get a twenty percent discount.'

A surprising number of people seemed delighted by this. Slim just gave a polite smile when Terrance's eyes passed across his.

Back on board, Alex took a back seat as Terrance stood in the boat's bow and waxed lyrical about fly fishing history, techniques, a few famous exponents of it, and some anecdotes about life as a fly-fisherman, in particular the surprising rivalry between fly-fishermen and traditional anglers, both of whom, for one reason or other, considered their discipline to be the most effective. Much of what Terrance said was lost in the buffering wind or broken by the calls of gulls trailing the boat, but one thing Slim did pick up was that fly-fishing was considered the more energy intensive of the two, requiring constant repeated casting, compared to regular angling, which, in Terrance's words, was a case of 'throw your hook out there then sit back for an hour with the Racing Post.'

After a half-hour ride back downriver, they chugged up a wide, slow-moving inlet and moored at a narrow jetty almost hidden by trees. Carrying gear handed to them by Alex as they climbed out of the boat, they followed Terrance Winters through the trees until they emerged on the shores of a diminutive reservoir which overflowed into one of the River Dart's tributaries. Some of the group seemed unhappy that they were practicing in a 'fishing pond' rather than the main estuary, but Terrance shrugged it off.

'As first-timers, you're far more likely to get a bite in relatively standing water. Successful fly fishing in flowing water takes years to master.'

No one seemed convinced, but few looked energetic enough to argue.

After a brief tutorial which involved much awkward holding of the rods and more than a few tangled lines, the guests were instructed to make a ring around the artificial lake about thirty feet apart. From there they were given freedom to attempt their own fly-casting, while Terrance walked in a clockwise circle, giving tips and corrections, with Alex walking the other way, asking inane questions and offering bottles of water to anyone who might have forgotten.

Slim, in a leafy spot out of sight of the guests to either

side of him, quickly realised that this labour-intensive version was not his preference. After Terrance's second appearance—by which time Slim had managed only one successful cast—he set his rod down and headed back into the undergrowth to where he had seen a sign pointing to a nearby viewing spot. Alex had also recently passed going the other way, and Slim estimated he had roughly thirty minutes before either man came by again.

The trail led up through forest, emerging after a brisk ten-minute hike onto a bald hilltop with a picturesque view of the Dart Estuary. A photo signboard gave names to the villages and inlets visible, short descriptions of some of the bird and plant life, and even a brief history of the industry on the river.

A knee-high barrier marked the edge of the safe area, but Slim stepped over it and went a few steps beyond until the hill's sudden drop-off revealed a view of the pier below where their boat was moored. Two other boats were moored alongside: a rowing boat, and a small motorboat with a cuddy over the wheel. As Slim watched, a stooped figure carrying a large hold-all appeared, walked up the pier and climbed into the motorboat. With the hum of an engine, it started out across the river.

Slim frowned, wondering what might have been inside the hold-all, then had a sudden moment of clarity.

'Alan McDonald,' he whispered. He had more of a desire than ever to speak with the local painter, if only to find out more about local customs and folklore. It might be meaningless, the stuff of storybooks, but it might—

Something shifted in the trees back where the path entered the clearing. Slim, his old military reflexes throwing him to the ground where he rolled behind a bench for cover, lost precious seconds as whoever had been spying on him got away. By the time he was up and running, crossing the clearing and ducking into the trees, the person was nothing more than a rustle of undergrowth farther down the slope.

Slim made his way down as quickly as he could, but whoever had been in the trees was either more trusting of the route down or more surefooted than he. By the time he reached the artificial lake, whoever it had been was long gone.

Aware his disappearance might soon be noted, he headed back to his place, arriving just as Terrance appeared through the undergrowth.

'Any luck?' he asked, giving Slim a smile, his reddened cheeks and the slight rasp to his breathing suggesting he was a little out of breath.

12

'Thanks, Don,' Slim said. 'I owe you one.'

'Any time,' Don said. 'Always happy to help.'

Slim frowned as he hung up, thinking about what Don had told him.

Carson, it transpired, was a man for whom both suicide and a hit would be equally likely. According to Don, who had several sources working inside tabloid newspapers, Carson's estranged wife had sold a story not only of multiple affairs, but one which involved both physical and mental abuse, and even elements of sadism. While Carson had taken his version of events to the grave, his wife's had been set to destroy whatever was left of his career before his unexpected death overshadowed everything.

And that was only the personal. Carson had debts, both gambling and drug related. He had joined the tour in Dartmouth as a way of putting some distance between himself and his creditors. Both they and the law were closing in, and like a circled outlaw, Carson had decided to go down in the only way he knew, with two potential trysts, and a bagful of booze and drugs.

The two unidentified women, not seen since the night of Carson's disappearance, could have easily been sent to perform a hit on him, aware that the idea of one last sexual adventure was not one a man of Carson's leanings could resist.

Slim shrugged and shook his head. It seemed too likely. The police could have gathered the same circumstantial evidence that he had, plus they had whatever had been found at the crime scene. If there had been foul play, they would have surely known.

Carson's feet were tied together, but it looked like he had done it himself.

Might it have been with a knife at his throat?

There were other options, of course. The first police on the scene, perhaps with vested interests—a family member with a business particularly reliant on tourism, perhaps—might have felt it necessary to conceal or spoil evidence to point the suspicion away from murder towards suicide. So much came back to the bonds on Carson's legs, but could they have been planted? If murder was considered, would some indication that Carson was a target be preferable to the idea of a random killer on the loose?

Slim's mind reeled with madcap ideas. He took a notepad from his bag and scribbled them down. Many of them were ludicrous, but the type that had helped him solve some mysteries previously deemed unsolvable. It was possible of course that he was fantasising over a simple suicide case, but the more he thought about it, the more his sense of paranoia grew. In his one short interaction with Carson, the DJ has come across as a person too arrogant to kill himself.

The very thought of suicide would have angered him. They would have had to cut him down where he stood.

And perhaps they had.

13

Slim skipped out on dinner. The thought of another evening of Eloise's threat-laden glares had stolen his appetite, so he stayed in his room until everyone would be seated, then headed down into Dartmouth. For once, as bright pub lights appeared through doorways on either side of the street, the thought of drinking was far from his mind. He carried on to the harbour, where he bought himself a bag of fish 'n' chips and sat on a promenade bench to eat. The sun had gone behind the hills and the long drawn out daylight of early summer was starting to fade. A couple of small fishing boats still moved up and down the river, but everything had an air of shutting down. The few sailors and fishermen he saw walked past him with slumped shoulders as though at the end of a long, tiring day.

After finishing his dinner and throwing the wrapper into a nearby bin, Slim reached into his pocket and took out a plastic card. Aware he was unlikely to get more information from the police, he needed to begin his own enquiry. A piece of red shoelace looped through a hole made with an office hole-punch. On one side was a slightly shadowy, less clean-shaven picture of Slim from the shoulders up. Against all identification photograph conventions, in the picture he wore a red baseball cap. The information alongside identified him as Mike Lewis, BBC Researcher. Below and on the back was some confidentiality and privacy policy jargon he had copied from the company's website.

Slim smiled. The card looked fake, but when you asked questions people wanted to answer, they tended to ignore it. Almost everyone, he had found, had an opinion on something, and gossip was a valuable currency, one which had bought him more leads than he cared to remember.

With the identity card strung around his shoulders, he assessed his options. He walked along the promenade a little way, looking at the line of shops, pubs and restaurants. He was wary of approaching locals because word might get around and information might dry up. Tourists, on the other hand, would probably know little, and would be more likely to go to the police if his questions upset anyone. The last thing he wanted was the police on alert that there was a man going about asking uncomfortable questions.

In the end, he headed for the most likely place he felt he could find information without word getting out: the fishing dock.

Dartmouth's jetties were predominantly for pleasure boats, but at one end, nestled below the headland on which the castle stood, was a wooden pier lined with small commercial fishing boats. Slim walked down to the end, but it seemed deserted, the moored boats bobbing gently in the water lapping against the pier's side.

He was just thinking of heading back to the hotel to get some sleep when he smelled something out of place.

Squatting down, he leaned closer to the pier's edge.

Over the top of the scent of salt water, fish, and even oil, was something pungent, flowery.

Lavender?

He leaned forward, peering over the edge. Something was down there, bobbing in the shadows at the very base of the pier wall, a small boat surrounded by flickering lights, something dark curled inside. The lights looked like candles ... and the lavender scent certainly came from there.

And the dark, curled shape looked like a—

Slim frowned. It couldn't be. He shifted forward another inch—

The lightest of touches on his back could have been hands, or merely a breeze gusting off the river. A clucking sound, which could have been maniacal laughter or a metal hook banging against a mast.

—then he was pitching forward, losing his balance, tumbling forward off the edge of the pier and down into the harbour below.

14

The doctor smiled. 'You're made of old leather, I'd suggest,' he said, patting the back of his clipboard. 'When I think about how far you fell ... you're very, very lucky, Mr. Hardy. The tide was out, exposing the rocks along the harbourside. That's a drop that might have killed you had there been nothing to break your fall.'

'What's the damage?' Slim said, attempting to push himself up in the bed, but finding one arm unresponsive. He groaned and gave up, slumping back into the pillow.

'Mostly cuts and bruises,' the doctor said. From his expression he was clearly trying to soften the blow by telling Slim the good news first. 'However, you've dislocated your left shoulder, the one you landed on. You cracked a couple of ribs on the edge of the boat, and you've sprained your right ankle. We're going to keep you in for a couple of days for observation, but by the weekend you'll be able to walk about. Your ankle will heal with a brace and your arm needs to stay in a sling, but in a couple of weeks you'll be back to your best. Just take it easy for a while.'

Slim nodded. 'Thank you. I appreciate you patching me up.'

'That's what we're here for.' The doctor's smile abruptly dropped. 'Now, if you're feeling up to it, the police are waiting to talk to you. They've been waiting outside all morning.'

Slim sighed and nodded. From what he remembered of last night's ordeal, it wasn't something he could avoid. 'You can send them in,' he said.

He recognised the two officers immediately. 'Hello again, Slim,' said WPC Oaks, taking a plastic chair, swinging it around and sitting down with it facing backwards. Slim had once thought such actions a staple of Hollywood movies only, until an old military friend had pointed out that the hard back of a chair made a decent shield against a desperate, lunging man.

The other police officer, PC Rogers, lingered by the door, one leg tucked behind the other, muscular arms folded.

'How much do you remember from last night?' WPC Oaks asked.

'All of it.'

'Talk me through it again in your own words.'

Slim took a deep breath, carefully reminding himself of which sections of the story he had altered, and which not.

'I didn't feel like eating with the other guests, so I went for a walk down through the town to the riverside, just to clear my head.'

'And you just happened to find yourself down by the old pier?'

'I didn't go straight there. I wandered around for a while, had something to eat. I was taking a stroll, that was all.'

'Quite a coincidence, don't you think?' PC Rogers said from the door, catching a scowl from WPC Oaks for his trouble.

'Go on,' she said.

'I smelled something strange, so I looked over the edge of the pier,' Slim said. 'I saw the candles down in the water … and that's when it happened.'

'You were pushed,' WPC Oaks said.

'I'm fairly sure of it.'

'But not certain?'

Slim grimaced. 'I could have been mistaken, but I don't think so.'

'You're an alcoholic, is that right?' PC Rogers said.

Slim gave a reluctant nod. 'But I haven't taken a drink in a couple of weeks. I was stone sober yesterday.'

'And then you fell?' WPC Oaks said.

'That's right.'

'And you landed on a rowing boat floating in the water?'

Slim gave a slow shake of his head. 'No. I landed on the body lying in it.'

'Irene Long.'

Slim sighed. 'Irene,' he said. 'I was speaking to her just hours earlier. I trust this is now a murder investigation?'

WPC Oaks didn't answer. Instead, she leaned forward and asked, 'Tell me what you remember next?'

'It hurt.'

'The boat was sitting in shallow water and you fell headfirst. It's likely you would have died had the boat not broken your fall.'

Slim closed his eyes, briefly imagining what it might have felt like to bash his head open on the rocks lying just below the surface. The give of the water and the soft, warm shape he had fallen on had kept him from serious harm.

'It was still warm,' he said. Then, regretful at referring to Irene as an object, he added, 'She ... she was still warm.'

'This is essential to our investigation,' PC Rogers said. 'The initial coroner's report has suggested that Irene Long died only a few minutes before you landed on top of her.'

'I imagine I contaminated the crime scene somewhat.'

WPC Oaks allowed a brief frown to give an indication of her true feelings.

'Somewhat is an understatement, I'm afraid. Forensics have to first remove whatever contamination you might have caused before looking for what might be beneath.' She fixed him with a stare. 'If indeed it is contamination.'

Slim nodded. 'So, I am a suspect. As I thought.'

'I can't give you a straight answer on that, but we're ruling nothing out at this point. The main point against you is why you happened to be in close proximity to Irene Long's body so soon after her death.'

'It was just bad luck. Or good, depending on your point of view.'

'Come on, Mr. Hardy,' PC Rogers said. 'Two people

from the same party are now dead. You were one of the last people to speak to the first, and you inadvertently discovered the body of the second.'

'And it's possible I was pushed,' Slim said. 'Shouldn't you be relieved it's two murders and not three?'

'We're aware of the situation,' WPC Oaks said, as PC Rogers rolled his eyes by the door. 'We're canvassing the town and investigating every possible lead, but there's not a lot to go on.'

'Why not?'

WPC Oaks watched him, eyes studying his face. Slim sensed the same intensity he had used on suspects in the past: that desperate need to remember every detail lest they be required later. She didn't have to say anything because he saw it in her gaze: he was a suspect. He had been in close contact with both victims shortly before their deaths, had no alibi for his whereabouts during the hours prior to either, and the way he had ducked out of an arranged dinner would have aroused their suspicions regarding his motives.

Very slowly, he said, 'Please be honest with me. I'm being treated as a suspect, aren't I?'

WPC Oaks ignored the question. 'Tell us what you remember of Irene Long,' she said.

'She seemed like a nice enough person—'

'I mean when you landed on her body.'

Slim swallowed. While he had seen plenty of corpses over the years, each experience was as traumatic as the last. Irene's had been no different.

'She was lying on her back,' he said. 'Her hands across her chest. Almost ... sacrificial.' As the two police officers exchanged a glance, Slim raised a weak hand. 'Can I ask a question?'

WPC Oaks shrugged. 'I'll hear it before I decide whether to answer it.'

'What was Irene's cause of death?'

'An overdose,' WPC Oaks said. 'Prescription medicine. We discovered her prescribed dosage was already dangerously high, so it can't have taken a lot to push it over the edge. We're currently having a blood analysis performed to establish exactly how much she had taken.'

Slim frowned, letting the information sink in. 'So, it could have been an elaborate suicide?'

WPC Oaks looked frustrated, as though nothing would suit her better than the hunt for a serial killer. 'That's how it appears. The boat would have been stolen had Mrs. Long actually gone anywhere. We believe she planned to drift out into the English Channel but died before she could set herself adrift.'

15

The next few days passed in a state of numbness. Even though the doctors told him he was free to move around provided he stayed in designated areas, he felt little motivation to get out of his hospital bed.

On Sunday morning, however, he had no choice when the doctor came to inform him he was due to be discharged.

'The arm has to stay in a sling for at least another week,' the doctor told him. 'And you need to visit your GP in a week or so to ensure there are no complications or resulting issues from the treatment. However, I think you'll be fine.'

'Thank you, Doctor.'

Slim spent an hour gathering his things, then headed downstairs with his appointment card tucked under his arm. In the lobby, he found Kim waiting in a plastic seat, halfway through a tatty Stephen King paperback.

'I really appreciate you picking me up,' he said. 'It's not really in your job description, is it?'

Kim smiled as she closed her book and put it away into a floral-patterned handbag. 'I don't actually have one,' she said. 'You never got around to writing it.'

'Probably a good thing.'

'Well, let's get going,' Kim said, standing up with a snap. 'I'm in short-stay and I don't think petty cash would handle a fine.'

'I thought you used that to keep me in coffee?'

Kim rolled her eyes. 'The other petty cash. Sometimes I wonder how you were ever successful enough to afford to hire me.'

'Blind luck,' Slim said. 'It kept me alive this week, too.'

'So I gathered. Shall we move along?'

Slim let Kim shoo him out into the car park, although he could only move as quickly as the crutch supporting his sprained ankle would allow. Kim's Nissan stood out because it was the only car which looked as though it had been washed that very morning. Kim helped him into the front passenger seat, then put the crutch into the back.

'Feel free to take a nap while I drive,' Kim said with a matronly lack of emotion, as she climbed into the driver's seat and started the car. 'I don't speed for any reason.'

He tried, but his mind was too clouded to relax. After an hour of staring out of the window, Kim pulled into the parking space outside Slim's flat.

'I cleaned up a bit,' Kim said. 'It was a terrible mess. Honestly, I don't know how you live like that.'

'Did I give you a key?'

Kim shrugged. 'It was in the top drawer of your desk.'

'Oh.'

'I do wish you'd be more careful, Mr. Hardy,' Kim said, picking up a kettle, then frowning at the water that burst from the tap with a pop of escaping air. 'In a certain way I have a fondness for you beyond even my salary. I don't want to see you dead.'

'I'll be all right.'

'Someone tried to kill you, Mr. Hardy.'

'There's a good chance. I can't be entirely sure. Either way, I appreciate the concern.'

'Have the police caught who did it yet? I saw Max Carson's death on the news and it was reported as a suicide. Have they updated their case yet?'

Slim shook his head. 'I've heard nothing. I keep expecting to be pulled in as a suspect, but I have no idea what they're thinking. All I know is that I'm deeper into this than I'd ever expected to be.'

⁓

After making him a cup of coffee and producing a casserole in a glass dish she had made before picking him up, Kim left. Alone again, Slim dumped an extra spoonful of instant into his coffee, microwaved it, and sat down at a desk by the window to consider what to do.

He had told Kim he planned to take a couple of weeks to recuperate from his injuries, but he had known when he said it that it was only an excuse to keep his schedule clear. She would be appalled at his plan, but the case of Max Carson and now Irene Long had caught him like an angler's hook, and there was no chance of it letting him go. Part of it was genuine interest, but there was definitely another part which had been left angered by the possible attack that had nearly left him dead. He had his suspicions, of course, but nothing concrete, nothing he could prove.

An hour later he arrived at the local bus station, limping a little on his bad ankle having left the crutch behind, a bag containing clean clothes and toiletries over his shoulder.

～

After a change in Exeter, he was back in the Dartmouth area just before nightfall. This time he stayed well clear of the main town, taking a room in a Travelodge on a fork off the main road, sandwiched between a Sainsbury's and the park-and-ride car park. He got something to eat in a downstairs restaurant populated by a few traveling businessmen, then went outside to familiarise himself with the local bus stops and timetables.

It was a ten-minute ride into Dartmouth. Slim had let his beard grow out since entering hospital, and now wore a battered wind-cheater, its hood pulled up, over old blue jeans. He got off at a central bus stop in front of the port. The last fishing boats had come in, and the area was quiet. He walked down the harbour side to the old pier where someone had made an attempt on his life. It felt strange to be back, the sling on one arm hidden beneath his jacket a reminder of how close he had come.

As he stood there, the wind ruffling his hair, his nostrils filled with the sour scent of fish entrails, a feeling came over him unlike any he had felt before. He had wondered what had truly brought him back here, when most people might never have dared return.

The longer he considered it, the more clearly he felt

The Angler's Tale

that feathery touch of hands on his back, helping him on his way over the edge of the fishing dock, and whoever had pushed him might not have realised at the time, but they had done something no one else ever had.

They had offered him a challenge.

16

Nearly two weeks had passed since the attempt on his life. Of course, the last guests from his tour had long since gone home, the remnants of the dark days of his stay only the two tour guides, Alex and Jane, whom he now watched through binoculars from the cover of the trees on the bank of the River Dart. The first excursion of the week was a general sightseeing trip, the boat setting off a little after nine and first heading out into the deep waters of the estuary, before turning and heading back upriver in the direction of Totnes.

With his jacket's hood pulled up, he had stood nearby, ostentatiously holding his phone to his ear while Alex made a gruelling twenty-minute welcome speech before the group embarked. After Totnes, they were planning a stop at Dittisham, where Slim could catch up by bus if he felt so inclined, but he had already gathered there was little information to be had.

Another week, another tour party. The trials of the last already dusted away.

Slim shrugged. As the boat went out of sight upriver, he packed up his things and headed back to the town.

Kingswear, directly across the river from Dartmouth, was a picturesque place occupying two sides of a hill jutting out into the river. A regular ferry operated between the two, while a number of small pleasure craft stood moored up in a small marina. Known as Dartmouth Harbour, several dozen other craft were moored to offshore piers. Slim caught a ferry across the river, then walked along the pier, idly looking at the pleasure boats that ran the gauntlet from Sunday hobby craft to multi-million pound yachts. From here, Dartmouth Castle was visible to the south, straddling a wedge of land near the river mouth.

He found a quiet café on one of Kingswear's back streets, slid into a booth and pulled a file out of his bag. Arranged in alphabetical order, it was background information on everyone he had recently come into contact with in the Dartmouth area, from Max Carson and Irene Long to fringe players such as WPC Oaks and PC Rogers. He had put both Kim and Don on the case, and the information included everything from press cuttings to print-outs of social media posts, responses and photographs. He was looking for connections, but the vast majority was of no interest whatsoever. Some profiles were less than a page long—Jane Hounslow, the tour rep, for example, had almost no online profile at all. All Kim had found was an old resume posted on a jobseeker's website in 2012, which listed her hobbies as baking and show-jumping. At the other end of the spectrum was Carson, who, among other things, was overly active on Twitter. From a quick skim through of the twenty-odd pages of printed tweets and replies, however, he liked to comment with no more than a couple of words or an emoji icon.

None of it was particularly useful. Slim concentrated his efforts on Carson and Irene, desperate to find some sort of connection, or even a reference to one, a shared interest in a particular company, for example, or even a particular place. But, despite his best efforts, he found nothing. They were polar opposites. Irene had posted more than two hundred pictures of a dog which—according to one last heartbreaking post—had been hit by a car in June, 2015. Carson, on the other hand, made no mention whatsoever of animals of any kind, and most of the pictures of him were dishevelled distance shots from the tabloid newspapers.

Slim, exasperated, ordered a fourth coffee, along with a cake which resembled a lump of sugar, since lunchtime was approaching. As he waited for the barista to pour his coffee, he looked over a rack of local business cards beside the counter.

Most were for tourist events and boat tours, but one was for an upcoming art exhibition in Totnes, showcasing local artists. Slim looked down a list of attending artists and saw a familiar name.

Alan McDonald.

Unusually for someone who sold his work in local shops, Slim had been unable to find out much about the man online. He had no website or social media page. The only references to him were in descriptions of a couple of original paintings for sale on eBay, one of which described him as "reclusive". Having seen the man out on his boat, Slim would hardly agree with the description, but Don had been unable to find a local address. Slim had asked around, but the best information he had received was 'he lives up in Totnes, but you'll see him about if you spend much time down the harbour.'

Since his return, Slim had seen nothing of the artist, but it might be about time to track him down.

17

Kingswear Station was the terminus of the Dartmouth Steam Railway, a seven-mile heritage railway which ran from Paignton to Kingswear, catering mostly to tourists. Slim's departure left at 15.30. He rode it as far as Greenway Halt, a small rural station with no ticket office, where he found himself the only person to get off. From there, he ignored a waiting shuttle bus and chose to walk instead, taking a pretty, meandering forest road with occasional views of the River Dart through the trees.

Despite being barely wide enough for two cars to pass, Slim began to encounter traffic on the road, moving in both directions. A couple of cyclists gave him a cheerful greeting as they passed, and once he had to wait while a group of American tourists took a photograph outside a low stone building set back from the road. A sign announced it as *Greenway Lodge - Holiday Lets*, and shortly afterwards he passed a welcome sign to *Greenway House - National Trust property*.

A short distance after that he came to an information board set into the grass verge.

Greenway House
The Summer Residence of Agatha Christie

He couldn't help but smile at the irony. That he would be so close to a legend of mystery fiction, while trying to solve his own, felt somehow appropriate.

The narrow lane wound away up ahead. Through the trees Slim glimpsed the angles of a white-walled manor house. He walked on a little farther, until he came to a footpath leading down into the trees. He paused, pulling a crumpled map out of his pocket. A cross drawn in biro seemed to match where he was standing. He stepped off the road and followed the trail downhill until it began to arc around, following the curve of the hillside. The Dart was visible through the trees, arcing around a last bend before straightening into Dartmouth Harbour. On the far bank, a car ferry was just pulling away from a pier.

Halfway down to the river, a smaller path broke off the main path. Slim took it, heading downhill. The path took him down through an old boathouse before rising up again. He sensed from his location that he was now on the south side of Greenway House, not far from an inlet the railway line had passed over via a bridge.

The main path continued on up towards the gardens at the rear of the house. Slim took out his map and examined it again, noting the location of the house and the X marked a little to the south. He walked to the nearest tree, then squatted down, feigning to tie a shoelace. As he did so, he glanced around, then closed his eyes and listened for the sound of footfalls. Certain he was alone, he stood up and stepped into the trees.

He was only pushing his way through leafy undergrowth for a minute or so before he emerged on a level section cut out of the hillside. Behind him it ended at a stand of trees that looked younger than the surrounding foliage, but ahead what appeared to be a carved path followed the contours of the hill. A little farther on Slim passed an outcrop of rock which still bore the scars of cutting equipment. Nearby, a dirty, sagging information board announced the path as an abandoned route for the Kingswear branch of the railway line. Slim wiped away accumulated dirt to read over the information, which detailed how in the 1920s, a post-war boom in tourism to the English Riviera had provoked a dramatic redevelopment plan to extend the riverside section of the Paignton-to-Dartmouth line. Several sections had been cut, a bridge half built, and even some gravel and sleepers laid down, but subsidence, fears of erosion, and rising costs had caused the plan's abandonment. As a way to cut losses, the train operator had sold a half-mile stretch of the track bordering Greenway to its owners at the time. When later, in 1938, Agatha Christie bought the estate, she had left the section of abandoned railway untouched.

Since taking over the property, the National Trust had blocked access to the section from the gardens. Slim was some way past Greenway now, which was above and behind him. The hillside curved around behind the house, then the trees dropped away as he approached the inlet river valley he had seen from the train. A line of police tape, appearing starkly out of place, hung between two trees, directly crossing the trail. Slim looked down, picked a path that wouldn't leave any boot prints, then circled around it, emerging from the trees on the other side.

A narrow valley stretched away to his left, cut by a river which spread into a marshy inlet below. The rusting iron frame of half a railway bridge stretched partway out across the boggy, reed-clogged water.

Slim took a deep breath, then walked out to the end and peered down.

The end section of the unfinished bridge, either collapsed under natural causes or destroyed for some reason, lay below, rusting metal bones of a giant decayed robot, part submerged, part overgrown. Little eddies flowed between pools where it had caused the river to back up, and the branches of a few gnarly trees bent and twisted through the metal slats.

Slim leaned out, looking straight down. Thirty feet, the police had said. It was enough to kill a man if you went headfirst and hit the metal rather than the sludge in between, but you could easily get trapped among the twisted metal and drown. It was clear where Carson had landed, because a section of the undergrowth had been cleared, exposing bare metal and boggy mud.

Slim sat down on the ground. Gravel covered the bridge's surface, dirt packed into a metal frame below. He looked back at the trees, noting the distance and the length of open space. A few thoughts came to mind he would write down later. First, how far it was back to the tree cover—a hundred feet at least. Second, how remote the location. It seemed inconceivable that Carson had found his way here by accident. Had he taken a tour of

Greenway he might have been aware of it, but there had been none on the early days of their itinerary and Carson hadn't come across as the National Trust type.

Secondly, that in the grey of pre-dawn, when Carson was estimated to have died, it would have been hard to surprise someone standing at the end of the severed section of bridge. Of course it was possible had Carson been intoxicated, but more likely someone had brought him here and thrown him over the edge.

Slim took a deep breath. He wondered what the police had thought as they stood here. Greenway was farther up the hill, invisible through the trees, and the small hamlet on the opposite riverbank was mostly out of sight around the bend. Only boats on the water that night could have seen him, or—

Slim paused. A tickle of irrational fear ran down his back. An old cottage stood back among the trees farther inland from the bridge, barely visible behind the screen of foliage that had grown up around it. The closer Slim looked, the more he realised it was tumbledown, its windows shattered or gone, its front door torn off and discarded. Branches threaded through holes gouged in the wooden walls.

Yet it looked familiar from somewhere. He retraced his steps back along the bridge and waded into the undergrowth that covered the hill right down to the waterside. There was no path here, no sign that the building had ever been accessible from this side. Too nervous to approach it directly, he circled around it like a cat assessing its prey.

It was larger than he had first thought. Rotting wooden outhouses stood to one side, while the cottage itself had a second floor hidden by overhanging tree branches. Glassless windows watched him as he clambered through the bushes.

He was staring at the dark, doorless space which led inside when the ground gave way beneath his foot. He fell, brambles scratching through his jacket, a nettle stinging as it encircled his wrist. He was nearer to the water's edge than he had realised. His foot had broken through the rotted remains of a jetty now buried in weeds and scrub.

He stood up and turned around, trying to imagine what it had been like before the collapsed bridge had created a makeshift dam and allowed the inlet to fill with silt and become marshland. With views downriver in the direction of the English Channel, it would have been charming, beautiful even. With the trees cut back, the views from the cottage's upper floor would have been even more impressive. Slim turned back to look again, in time to catch movement in one of the upper windows. A dose of freezing terror rushed through him and he caught a momentary glimpse of an old woman standing there, leaning against the window frame, the fingers of one hand visible as they curled around the wall. Even after he realised it was only a shred of ancient curtain blowing in the breeze, the fear refused to abate until he turned away and slowly began to make his way back to the old train line.

18

From a local library, Slim checked out what nonfiction books on Agatha Christie and the history of the Greenway estate he could find, and retreated to the café in Kingswear to go over them. Not being much of a reader, he found them a hard slog, but passing off the job to Kim would reveal his intentions. He was officially on sick leave, he reminded himself. One book, however, had a glossary at the back which made references to Greenway easy to find. The few brief mentions had little substance though, stating merely that it had been a holiday home for the Christie family and that Agatha had been happy there. He found no mention of the tumbledown cottage.

Frustrated, he caught the ferry across to Dartmouth, where he spent an hour browsing tourist shops, picking up another couple of local history pamphlets. Returning by bus to his hotel, he read them over dinner, but again found little of substance. The only mention of the abandoned section of railway said just that: it had been abandoned due to fears of erosion and rising costs. There was no mention of the bridge, the house, or any connection to Greenway. Slim tossed the books aside. It was possible he had got everything wrong, and that there was no connection between the deaths of Carson and Irene Long, that both had been elaborate but undisputed suicides. The bridge was a collapsed bridge, the house an old house, the connection to the former home of a famous mystery writer pure coincidence.

Unable to sleep, he sat at the room's desk and began poring over the information Donald Lane had sent him, but found nothing of interest. No connections, nothing, just a list of isolated individuals who had nothing to do with each other.

He shook his head. Perhaps he was going mad. Perhaps there really was nothing to find and he was chasing ghosts.

Ghosts.

The word floated around his head like an embodiment of its meaning. No doubt Max Carson and Irene Long had been haunted in their separate ways, but the longer he considered it, the more real the hands that had tried to push him over the pier's edge had been.

Whatever the police believed, there was a killer out there, or at the very least, someone who wanted to be.

He was sure of it.

19

Early morning, with rain threatening overhead, Slim walked into Dartmouth, his hood pulled up to hide his identity. Most businesses were just opening up. The ominous clouds had kept the tourists away, so Slim made a circuit of the main shopping area, mentally noting any shops likely to be of interest, then cycled back to begin at the first one he had seen.

The shopkeeper, a middle-aged woman with her hair tied up in a flower-patterned scarf, looked up as he entered.

'If you need anything, give me a shout,' she called, before returning to opening a box of key rings hung with metal cutouts of Dartmouth Castle.

'Actually,' Slim said. 'There is something.'

He reached into a coat pocket and pulled out a small ziplock bag. Inside was a square of fabric he had cut from the back of an old sweater, the one he had been wearing the night he had fallen off the pier to land on Irene Long's funeral barge.

It hadn't felt right to keep the sweater, but the patch he had cut free retained a residue of scent from one of the candles or incense burners on the boat. Slim, who considered the best form of perfume to be a shower, wasn't able to identify it, but he hoped to track down where it had come from. As the shop assistant came over, Slim held up the square of fabric.

'This might seem like a strange thing to ask,' he said, 'but I'm trying to find out what happened to my sister. You see, she recently died in mysterious circumstances, and the police aren't giving me much information.'

'Oh, I'm very sorry to hear that,' the woman said. 'I suppose that's no surprise. Not like the police to keep things to themselves, is it? How can I help?'

'I wondered if you had anything for sale that smells like this?' he said, indicating the fabric. 'This scent was on her body when she died.'

'Oh, that's a little morbid. I mean, I'm sorry, I don't mean it like that, I mean—'

Slim smiled. 'It's fine,' he said. 'We weren't close. I just want to know what happened to her, that's all.'

'Well, I suppose you would, wouldn't you?'

The woman looked a little disconcerted, but she took the material and smelled it anyway. She frowned, then shrugged.

'We have a few scented candles over here,' she said, indicating a sales rack near the window loaded with colourful candles and incense sticks, some of a beach design, the wax infused with sand, shells, or pretty stones, others East Asian or floral-patterned. 'I don't recognise that smell, though. I don't think it's one of ours.'

Slim humoured her for a while as she allowed him to

check for himself, but in truth, to Slim one chemical fragrance smelled much like another. Confident the woman couldn't help him, he thanked her and left, moving on to the next shop he had scoped out. He found no luck there or at the next, but at the fourth place he tried, a woman seemingly so old she could barely lift herself out of her chair behind the counter looked up at him through glasses obscuring one blind eye, and reached out a gnarled hand to receive the shred of fabric.

Afraid repeated exposures would reduce the fabric's scent to nothing, he had little confidence, but the old woman took one sharp sniff, looked up at him and nodded.

'Over there. Second box up, the blue ones.'

'You're sure?'

Slim went to look, retrieving a couple of scented candles. Lavender and rosehip. It was hard for him to notice a similarity in smell even with the candles in hand, but the old woman was nodding. 'Your sister bought some of these, did she?'

'I believe so, yes. I'm trying to trace her last movements. Are these only sold here?'

The old woman shrugged, then winced as though the gesture were painful. 'How would I know? Might be sold in another shop. We did sell a couple to a girl the other week. Not big sellers, these, so it's easy to remember.'

'A girl?'

'Young maid. Wouldn't go so far as call her pretty. Had these crazy eyes, looked like she was on something. If she'd had a bag I might have thought she was fingering the goods, but she went straight to those candles like she knew what she wanted.'

'Crazy eyes?'

'Yeah, and long brown hair, wavy at the bottom as though it didn't agree with the sea air.'

Slim gave a thoughtful nod. 'Thankful for your time,' he said, then left.

Outside, Slim took a deep breath. Crazy eyes. Long brown hair, wavy at the bottom. It wasn't a description of Irene, but one of Eloise.

20

Totnes was less picturesque but more functional than Dartmouth with a larger shopping centre and better regional transport links. Following signs from the ferry pier, Slim found his way to the small riverside exhibition hall converted out of a former warehouse.

Renovated but retaining the vintage charm of its working days, the building was now a modern arts space and contained a small cinema listing several movies Slim had never heard of, plus a café and a number of exhibition rooms. A temporary sign announced an exhibition titled *Views of the River*, housed in a narrow room at the end.

Near the door was a table set up with painting equipment, where a local painter was giving tips to two young children while their mother looked on with interest.

A nametag identified the painter as Bill Sheckles. He looked up as Slim entered, smiled, and gestured towards the exhibits. Slim wandered through, only vaguely interested in the paintings, most of which were landscape views of the Dart and her estuary from a variety of hilltop angles, mixed with still-lifes of moored boats and views of Dartmouth Castle. His interest wasn't piqued until he reached a section near the back comprised solely of views from the water itself.

An information card explained that the section was dedicated to local painter Alan McDonald. It gave a brief bio, informing Slim that Alan had been born in 1933 in Dartmouth and had worked as a fisherman most of his life before dedicating his retirement to his other passion, painting. His familiar habit of painting from a boat was favoured due to a vessel's comforting rocking compared to the rigidity of painting on dry land. He was quoted as saying, 'I'm a child of the river. I was born on water and will likely die on it. I've always been suspicious of dry land.'

Most of the paintings were hard to differentiate, multiple angles of the same picturesque views. Many were great swathes of choppy water, given form by the ripples left by a boat's wake or the mottled colour of a passing watercraft. Others were framed by distant riverbanks, loaded with towns and hills, or of inlets with triangles of water giving way to rolling hills, clusters of houses, private jetties, the odd snaking road leading out of the valley. Slim had hoped for more views of the tumbledown house or the old woman watching the river with her arms crossed, but found none.

Aside from Bill and the family by the entrance, Slim was the only person present. There was no sign of Alan McDonald, so Slim waited until the children were done with their painting lesson and sauntered over to Bill.

'I'm looking for Alan McDonald,' he said. 'Is he around? I bought one of his paintings the other day and was hoping to meet him.'

'You and me both,' Bill said with a look of frustration. 'He should be here by now but he's late. Everyone knows he was upset that his paintings were curated, but he's been sulking about it. He didn't show up to the prep meeting yesterday, so whether he'll come at all is anyone's guess.'

'Do you have an address for him?'

Bill laughed. 'Of course not. He's private about that stuff. He uses his mother's address for correspondence but he doesn't live there. Just stops in once in a while to pick up his post.'

'Do you have hers?'

Bill shook his head. 'I don't, but Len, who's in this evening, might. If you come back about five o'clock?'

Slim grimaced. He would miss the last ferry back to Dartmouth and he wasn't in the mood for expensive taxi rides.

'You say Alan should be in today?'

Bill checked his watch. 'Half an hour ago.'

'Thanks,' Slim said. 'I'll take a wander about and check back in a while.'

'I wouldn't get your hopes up,' Bill said. 'He's not very social.'

Slim humoured Bill with a smile and headed out. He wandered the riverside for a while, before the exhibition hall's café inevitably reeled him in. The coffee was too bright and breezy for his liking, but it was a pleasant day, and, sitting on a picnic table on the grass outside the exhibition hall as the warm sun tickled his face, he could overlook that the water in his cup had likely only met coffee for a fleeting moment. Wincing with each sip, he stared out at the river.

He had been sitting there no more than a couple of minutes when a short, bustling figure came hurrying past, an overlarge bag under one arm, a handkerchief in his other hand which sporadically mopped his face. His cheeks were sun-reddened and he wore a floppy cricket hat. Even if his very awkwardness coupled with a stumbling, land-weary gait hadn't made him stand out, the flecks of paint on his trousers and shirt would have identified him. With a last reluctant glance over his shoulder at the river, the figure headed into the exhibition hall. Slim poured the rest of his coffee out on the grass, then gathered up his things and went to speak with Alan McDonald.

21

Bill had gone. In his place, Alan sat behind a desk by the entrance, his eyes darting around, looking like he'd rather be anywhere else but here. The mother and her children were gone too, and besides one middle-aged man browsing near the back of the room, pulling off spectacles to peer closely at a painting of a rowing boat sitting on a triangle of sand near a harbour wall, the exhibition room was empty.

'Excuse me,' Slim said. 'Are you Alan McDonald? I've been hoping to meet you.'

The man ignored him for a few seconds as he mixed a couple of paints together in a small plastic pot, his hand stirring nervously.

Slim was about to repeat his request when the man looked up.

'Thank you for coming,' he said, his voice containing a slight tremble. 'Why don't you take a look around?'

'I already did,' Slim said. 'There's some fine work here. The real reason I wanted to talk to you was because

I bought one of your paintings the other day. It's an excellent piece. I think I'm becoming something of a fan.'

Some of Alan's obvious social awkwardness seemed to ease. 'That's kind of you to say. Which piece, if you don't mind me asking?'

'One of the railway line below Greenway,' Slim said. 'Just as it crosses a bridge over an inlet.'

Alan's smile dropped. 'The ghost train,' he said. 'What made you want that one?'

'It's beautiful,' Slim said. 'Your work is masterful. It really caught my eye.'

'Well, thank you.'

'Why did you call it a ghost train?'

Alan shrugged. 'It was more of an imaginative piece. No trains ever ran on that section of the line. That bridge isn't even standing now.'

'I know. I went out there yesterday.'

Alan looked away. He fiddled with his paints, frowning at the same time. His cheeks reddened as though from exertion, and a grim smile came over his face.

'I prefer to remember it—there, that place—as it should have looked,' he said.

'You mean, before someone died jumping off the end of that bridge?'

Alan looked up briefly, then looked away again, fiddling even harder with his paints. A splash of green-blue flicked across his jacket but he appeared not to notice.

'Are you from the police?' he asked, not looking up.

Slim shook his head. He had considered what he might say to Alan if they managed to meet, and went for the safe option, what he considered a gentle bending of the truth.

'I was visiting Dartmouth on holiday a few weeks ago,' he said. 'I was part of a tour group. Sadly, another member of the same party committed suicide. I had the unfortunate distinction of being the last known person to see him alive.'

Alan looked up, narrowing his eyes, and for a moment Slim felt certain the old angler was filling in the blanks in Slim's story.

'The radio man,' he said at last.

'Max Carson was a well-known DJ,' Slim said. 'Many would call him infamous.'

'I heard some rumours, but I don't watch television or read newspapers,' Alan said. 'It's all just bad news, isn't it?'

Slim shrugged. 'For the most part. I don't think there's much to report. I just wondered about it, that's all. I saw your painting in a local shop in Dartmouth, and I liked it. What surprised me was that the assistant appeared to be taking it off sale.'

Alan waved the hand holding the paintbrush and a little more watercolour splashed over his shirt. 'I suppose they can do what they like with their displays,' he said.

'Then there was another I saw in a coffee shop. It was a lovely painting of an inlet, and an old house with a woman standing outside. I could almost imagine it was the same old house that's not far from the bridge, although there was no railway line in that one.'

'Probably another imaginative piece. The mind tends to wander out there on the water.'

'I don't doubt it. What I noticed was that the woman

and the house had been covered by a stack of books. I'm sure I'm chasing shadows, but I wondered why. I thought that if anyone had any ideas, it would be the person who painted both pictures.'

'Me?' Alan said, as though about to deny any knowledge of them. 'I'm just a painter, that's all.'

'You're also a local person, and, without meaning to be rude, you've been around a long time. You must have an opinion on it all.'

'On what?'

'On what it is about that railway bridge, that old house, maybe even that woman. I mean, Max Carson is supposed to have killed himself, yet that location is remote. He'd have been better off jumping in front of a train or throwing himself off the cliffs around Dartmouth Castle. Why there?'

Alan shifted uncomfortably. 'This is not a conversation I want to have,' he said. Three middle-aged women wearing matching yachting club t-shirts came through the door and Alan practically jumped out of his seat to greet them, leaving Slim standing awkwardly by the painting table. He waited, but Alan looked intent on giving them an impromptu tour of the gallery.

Frustrated, Slim headed out, aware that the café had a view of the exhibition room's entrance. He took a seat near a window into the lobby area and got to work going through the profiles Don had sent him, no longer looking for connections but turning his attention back to another unsolved mystery among many: who might have attempted to kill him by pushing him over the edge of the pier.

At a shade under six feet and a dead hundred

kilograms on the last occasion he had checked, it would have taken a brave person to attempt to push him over the edge, had he not done most of the work for his assailant by leaning over to look into the water directly below. Now he looked at it logically, the attempt on his life had been opportunistic. His assailant couldn't have known his plans, but must have been following close behind and pounced on the opportunity when Slim let his guard down.

At a flicker of movement at the edge of his vision, Slim looked up. Outside the café window, Bill Sheckles was waving at him. Slim jumped up, aware that Alan would be due to finish his shift, but by the time he made it out of the café and around to the exhibition's welcome desk, Bill was standing with his hands on his hips and a look of annoyance on his face.

'He skipped out early,' he said. 'The lazy sod. I should have known better than to trust him to keep an eye on things.'

22

Alan's motorboat was gone by the time Slim reached the riverside. Frustrated at fluffing his chance, he took a ferry back to Dartmouth. By the time he stepped off the boat onto the tourist pier, a cold breeze was blowing in off the English Channel. Even though daylight would last a few more hours, the few people on the streets looked keen to find shelter.

Pulling his jacket right around him, Slim bought a bag of chips and sat shivering beneath a bus shelter as the grey clouds that had rolled in during his journey back began to dispense their load, the rain clattering on the concrete around him.

To his dismay he had missed the last bus which would take him up to the main road and his hotel, leaving him with an expensive taxi journey or a tough uphill walk. He stared straight ahead as he ate, ignoring the rain as his thoughts drifted back to the night his life had been saved by Irene Long's dead body.

It was impossible that there couldn't be a connection

between the three events, and he kept returning with reluctance to another face on the periphery of everything, one that made him uncomfortable to think about.

Eloise.

Finishing his chips, he pulled out the file of character profiles, flicking through until he found the girl's.

Eloise Tiffany Trebuchet, a family name which had come from French and was pronounced with an accent. None of what the girl had claimed was backed up by a social media presence which was painfully brief. Slim had hoped for dirt on a girl who had claimed to have left a man for dead, but if Don couldn't get it, it likely didn't exist. Could it really be possible that the girl was some kind of outpatient from a psychiatric institution? If she was, there had to be a record, unless she was using an assumed name.

Slim stared at the print in front of him. He had caught her following him and she matched the description of the woman seen buying the candles which had later shown up on Irene's funeral barge. But there was little else. She had an address in Exeter, a job at a local telecoms company. No listed family or friends, and a handwritten comment from Don said he'd had no luck tracking any down. Her online contacts were work colleagues or randoms, friends of friends or perhaps even people she'd never met. Her profile picture had been touched up by a photo editor, Don claimed. The high percentage of male associates suggested a girl looking for a partner, yet Don had searched through what online matchmaking sites he knew and hadn't found her.

Could the feather-light touch he remembered on his

back have come from the girl? The attention she had shown him and her random appearances suggested she had been following him.

It was hard to be sure if he had felt anything at all, and the immediate aftermath of crashing onto a dead woman lying in a rowing boat had stolen the best part of his recollection. It was possible.

Which, of course, led to another question. Why? Sharp and threatening she had been, but Slim had done her no personal slight except perhaps misreading the signs for some skewed sexual advance. She had the look of a person who could develop a grudge from nowhere, but even so, Slim had no idea how he might have caused one.

But, if he had … he needed to know. Don hadn't found out much about her, but he had tracked down a workplace.

The rain still poured, making the toes of his boots slick and shiny. Slim twisted around to look at the bus timetable.

There, on the second chart down among a list, was a recently added direct bus to Exeter.

∽

The witching hour. So it was called, Slim had heard, as he wandered Dartmouth's streets in the damp, chilly air after a local church bell tolled the twelve strokes of midnight. Except for a handful of stumbling tourists, he saw no one, and soon, as the last peals of drunken laughter died away behind the slammed doors of holiday lets, he found himself alone.

Dartmouth after midnight looked exactly as he should have expected: like a quiet port town closed down for the night.

Except it wasn't really closed. Slim, standing by the riverside, heard the gentle hum of an engine as a small fishing boat arrived to unload its catch or perhaps collect supplies before heading back out.

He walked along the quayside until he was level with the pier where the boat was coming in. Shadows were everywhere. As a fisherman jumped off the boat to secure it to a mooring post, Slim stepped off the pier, lowering himself into a space between a bobbing motorboat and the quayside. A rail on the outer side allowed him a handhold, and he clung to the boat's hull like a barnacle, his shoes just above the water line, his elbows hooked over the rail, the shadows and his black clothes concealing him.

He had trusted to luck that there would be more than one fisherman working the boat and he was right. There were three, two with strong Westcountry accents and a third who sounded like a London import. Feeling like he'd come right back to his second night in Dartmouth, he listened to them work as they unloaded lobster pots onto the quayside.

After a couple of minutes, Slim learned their catch was due in an Exeter fish market in barely three hours' time. As the Londoner headed off to 'bring the van around', however, one of the others paused to spark up a cigarette.

'Davey, I thought you quit.'

'Yeah, me too.'

'Kelly giving you grief about another kid?'

A nervous laugh. 'Something like that. Hey, I thought you didn't drink, Frank.'

'We all have our poisons, Davey.'

'That wasn't her, was it?'

'Nah. Light reflecting off the water.'

'Yeah.'

Both men fell quiet. Slim imagined them partaking in their respective vices in a quiet moment of thought.

'I've never noticed any windows in that place,' Davey said at last. 'Just the holes. And the reflection ... I mean, what from? There's nothing across the water.'

'Could've been the moon.'

'It's not that bright. Someone was in there, I'd swear on my mother's grave.'

Frank gave a cold laugh. 'Give you a fifty if you drive out there right now and check it out. Mick'll be back with the van in a sec. We can drop you off. Make a vid on your phone to prove it.'

'Not much chance of that.'

'Wouldn't you want to know if Old Bea's come back? I mean, she got that guy, didn't she?'

'Don't make me laugh. Guy probably did it himself. I heard he did it to make sure. He went head down, would have drowned in the sludge even if the fall didn't kill him.'

'You shouldn't believe everything you hear in the pub.'

Davey gave a wry chuckle. 'Neither should you. Hey, here's Mick.'

So, we're dropping you off, is it?'

'Screw yourself.'

They walked off together, carrying lobster pots, along

the pier in the direction of an idling van, its rear lights glowing in the darkness. Slim waited until they had loaded the van and climbed in, before pulling himself up over the quayside's wall and massaging warmth back into his aching muscles. He walked up the pier as the van pulled away, turning out onto the main road.

Lights in the tumbledown house. Old Bea. He had heard that expression before, but whereas previously it had slipped past, now it glowed like the lights of a fishing boat in the night.

23

The journey to Exeter, at barely an hour and a half, wasn't long enough to either warm Slim's body after a night outside, nor provide enough sleep to make up for what he had missed. He stumbled off the bus, found a café and dozed in a window booth until a staff member came over and asked him to leave.

It didn't take long to figure out that the address of Eloise's workplace given on the internet was out of date. When Slim arrived, he found an empty office building, windows painted over, doors secured by a chain. He visited the neighbouring premises in a hunt for information, but those who didn't eye his appearance with disdain claimed to know nothing.

He was feeling at a dead end when he noticed a dank pub around the corner and decided to canvass it for information.

The pub wasn't yet open, but when Slim leaned through a door left ajar and enquired about a coffee, the landlord beckoned him inside and gestured to the stools lined along an unlit bar. Seemingly happy for some company, the landlord made small talk with Slim while he finished arranging furniture and wiping tables. When he went to pour away the dregs of yesterday's coffee pot in order to make a fresh one, Slim told him it would do fine.

'If it was two days old, even better,' he said.

'Not seen you round here,' the landlord said, introducing himself as Jack Hodges. Grey hair around his ears and a couple of liver spots on his forehead put him in his mid-fifties, although he was slimmer than was usual for a man who worked a bar, suggesting a late career change or a healthy lifestyle outside his occupation. 'And not a lot of tourists stray this far from the cathedral.'

'I'm looking for Comtel Solutions,' Slim said. 'I'm on the trail of an old friend I believe worked there. According to the address I have, it should have been in that building right across the street.'

Jack nodded. 'Yeah, there was an office of sorts there for a while. Were a few in there at one point but the council did the landlord for faulty wiring and the place got cleaned out. Gutted my lunchtime trade, although not many used to stick around of an evening.'

'You often encountered the staff?'

Jack gave half a shrug. 'They were office suits, and there's nowhere else in walking distance.'

'Do you know what happened to the company?'

Jack shook his head. 'No idea, sorry.'

'And when did it close?'

'Oh, a year or so ago. It was early summer I think. Last year. You said you were looking for a friend?'

Slim nodded. 'More of an acquaintance. A girl. Early twenties. Long hair, slight curl at the bottom, thin, eyes a bit too wide to make you comfortable. Her name was Eloise.'

Jack had been in the process of splitting open a bag of crisps to pour into a bowl between them, but now he paused. Slim noticed a slight tremble in his hands, one that could have mirrored many of his own.

'You know her, don't you?'

Jack stared at the floor. His mouth creased and he gave a little sigh.

'Are you police?'

Slim laughed. 'God, no. I'm just trying to track her down. You do know her, don't you?'

'I did,' he said. 'Briefly.'

'Can you tell me about it?'

Jack turned suddenly, crossing his arms, adopting a defensive posture. 'Look. Who the hell are you, and why do you want to know about this girl?'

Slim reached into his pocket and pulled out a business card. It was crinkled from being sat on and had a little rip on one corner. He laid it on the bar with the name turned towards Jack.

'I'm a private investigator,' he said. 'John Hardy. People call me Slim.'

Jack picked up the card and turned it over in his hand. 'Not a successful one if this is anything to go by.'

Slim shrugged. 'I have my moments. My secretary made this for me. She said I ought to have one. Make me look more professional than I really am.'

His self-deprecation lowered Jack's guard. The landlord sighed, then pulled a glass from under the counter and poured himself a measure of vodka from a bottle hung over the bar. At the smell, Slim felt a sudden lurch in his stomach. He gripped the edge of the bar, hoping Jack wouldn't notice.

'What do you want Eloise for?' Jack asked, lifting the vodka and downing it in one swallow. As he put the glass on a counter behind him, out of Slim's reach, Slim let his fingers relax.

'A couple of weeks ago, I think she tried to kill me,' he said.

24

Exeter County Council resided in a bland modern rectangle out of keeping with some of the more historical buildings nearby. Slim, still stunned by Jack's confession, headed inside and found his way to the commerce and trading department.

'Comtel Solutions,' he told the clerk at the front desk. 'I'm trying to get a high court writ on uncollected debt,' he added, working on the lie he had brainstormed on the way over. 'All I need to know is if they went bankrupt or simply changed premises.'

'Sure,' the clerk said. 'Let me check the paperwork we have on them.'

Slim took a seat in a waiting area as the clerk disappeared through a door into an inner office. He stared, his eyes glazed, at a TV in a corner with its sound down low, remembering Jack's words and wondering if he was on the trail of a psychotic killer.

'They had some kind of after-work party in here one night, six of them,' Jack said, pouring himself another measure. He looked about to offer one to Slim, then appeared to notice how Slim clutched the edge of the bar as he stared at the glass. He swallowed it as he had done before then put the glass out of range.

'It was clear right away that she wasn't popular, that perhaps they didn't want her there. After a couple of hours they did a runner on her while she was in the bathroom. It didn't go down well and she stormed out after them. A couple of minutes later she was back, wanting another drink. We talked awhile. There was no one in that night so around ten I decided to close early and offered her a lift home.'

'And one thing led to another?'

'Believe it or not, I had no plans for it. She unnerved me to be honest, but at some point something was said and she ended up back at mine.' Jack gave a sheepish grin. 'I mean, why wouldn't I? My wife's been dead ten years and I've been alone ever since. The girl was half my age at least and attractive enough if you could get past that glare.'

Slim was in no position to take a moral high ground. He smiled in agreement then nodded at the near-empty coffee pot. 'I'll take whatever's left of that,' he said. 'What happened?'

Jack chuckled, but the sheen in his eyes betrayed a horror being recalled.

'I live a ways across town. She named a place nearby but halfway there told me her parents had kicked her out and she had nowhere to stay. I offered her my sofa, but you know, let's not play this like a film. I wasn't about to pressure her, but I wouldn't have turned her down if an offer came. I sleep alone enough as it is.'

'And one did?'

Jack sighed again. 'I don't remember what words were said, but yeah, we ended up in bed. I'll hold her modesty there, if you don't mind. That part went ... well, good. It was afterwards that things changed.'

'There's more?'

'Sorry.' Jack poured himself a third drink. As Slim watched the clear liquid slide down the man's throat, he could barely control himself.

'Want one?' Jack asked.

Slim, his throat dry, said, 'Actually, it's the last thing I want.'

Jack gave a knowing nod. 'Say no more. Well, the long and short of it is I woke sometime in the middle of the night with a knife pressed against my throat.'

'She attacked you?'

'Not in a certain sense. I remember my neck having this numbing coldness as though she'd been sitting there with the knife pressed against it for some time. I tried to flinch away but she'd wrapped the duvet around me in a way that prevented me from moving. I couldn't do anything. I've never been so scared in all my life.'

Jack shook his head. Slim waited, knowing there was more. Finally Jack said, 'I couldn't say a word. I look back on it now and a million better ways to react come into my mind, but at the time I was helpless.'

'Did she say anything?'

'Only one thing. She said, "You don't know who I am." That's it. Then she moved the knife away from my neck and laid it across the duvet. I still didn't move. She stood up, walked to the door and went out. I could have grabbed the knife at any time, but I felt paralysed. Even after I heard the front door open and close, and her footsteps on the path outside, I didn't move. Believe it or not, I actually fell asleep again. When I woke up it was morning. I'd twisted out of the duvet in the night and was clutching the knife in my hand. I never saw her again after that. She was never with the other staff from that company who occasionally came in for a drink, and I couldn't bring myself to ask. Until you walked in asking about her, I'd managed to convince myself that I'd just had a really vivid dream.'

'You didn't go to the police?'

Jack sighed and shook his head. 'No. No, I didn't.'

∽

The clerk was calling Slim over. He shook off the fugue of memory and made his way over to the desk.

'Comtel Systems went into liquidation six months ago,' the clerk said, passing him a piece of paper. 'This is all the information on record.'

Slim nodded and thanked the clerk, then took the piece of paper and slid it into his pocket. Outside, he found a park bench and read over it.

A freedom of information document, with the details of the company and its ownership. He had another name now: Leon Davids, CEO. He found a local library nearby where he could use a computer. There, he looked up Davids online, but as he opened a page and scrolled down, he shook his head in disbelief.

Leon Davids was dead. The cause of death: suicide.

25

Slim waited until he was back at his hotel before he called Don. He had found nowhere online which gave a location or a rationale for Leon Davids' death, but Don had lines of investigation few others had. His old army friend promised to get back to him in a day or two with whatever he could find out about the circumstances.

Too wired to sleep, Slim went downstairs, found a computer in the hotel lobby and spent some time looking for any updates about the case of the suicides. Of Carson, however, there were only the initial reports he had already seen, and there was nothing at all related to Irene, as though her death had been swept under the constabulary carpet.

He was facing a dead end. Without a decent lead he would soon be forced to give up and admit he had finally come upon a case he couldn't break open.

He wanted to scream, or at least bash in the computer screen. Neither was a good option if he wanted to keep his hotel room.

Sadly, there was a third option. Through a door a short way past the alcove of computer terminals was the hotel bar.

The old cravings had been strong since his meeting with Jack. Slim stood up, switched off the computer, and went to get a drink.

~

'Excuse me? Sir? Excuse me?'

Slim opened his eyes and a wave of pain and regret came flooding in. Something hard pressed into his stomach; after a moment he realised it was the desktop of the lobby computer terminal where he must have chosen to crash for the night.

'You can't sleep there, sir. I'm afraid I have to ask you to return to your room or I will have to call the manager.'

'The manager?' Slim groaned, trying to sit up. The blazing lights of the hotel lobby cut a path through his drunkenness like a spotlight through the dark. The clerk was too close, his voice too loud, the whites of his eyes too large. When the man blinked, his eyelids snapped shut with a clapperboard clack.

'Sir? Could you look at me please, sir?'

Slim lurched upright. As he nudged a computer mouse the screensaver cleared, revealing an open messenger email box. Slim stared at the TO: name over the top and let out a relieved sigh that the box was empty. Then he noticed the SENT box at the bottom. His heart sank at the sight of the first two lines of a badly spelled and punctuated message.

'Sir? Please, sir—'

'All right.' Slim hastily closed down the open window. He tried to get up off the chair, but stumbled and somehow managed to sprawl across the floor at the clerk's feet.

'Sir? I can call someone to assist you—'

'I can manage!' Slim snapped, pushing himself up, aware how ungainly he must appear, but pleased that it was late at night with no other customers around. His bag lay nearby so he grabbed it and stumbled away from the computer cubicles, past the entrance to the now-closed bar.

In the reception area, another clerk was talking on the phone, a worried expression on his face. Slim made a quick assessment of the situation. He had paid for a week in advance, and that week wasn't yet up. He owed no money, and had everything of importance to him in the bag at his side.

He didn't need to face the police right now.

'I'm checking out,' he said, waving his bag towards the door. 'Thank you. I enjoyed my stay.'

Without looking back, he shouldered his bag and headed out into the night. As he walked across the parking area towards the bus stop he glanced back. Several staff members watched him from the entrance.

Had he overreacted? Maybe so, but he couldn't recall what he might or might not have done. He knew, however, as he reached the bus shelter with the timetable sandwiched between two plates of glass, that it was either too late or too early to get transport anywhere. Instead, he simply carried on walking, wondering, as the darkness closed in around him, which was more likely: he was now homeless, a fugitive, or both.

26

It wasn't long before his phone started to ring. First was the inevitable: Kim, no doubt annoyed at being pulled from her bed at such an ungodly hour, was unable to hide the frustration behind her concerned message. She demanded that he get in contact, and had the voicemail not cut off, Slim suspected it may have been followed by a threat of resignation.

The next three calls were all from the same number. The first two hung up quickly, but the third went to voicemail. Waiting until it cut off, Slim listened in alarm to the voice of a police officer, urging him to pick up. They were worried about him, concerned for his safety. Slim knew the drills, however. They wanted to reel him in.

It seemed that walking out of a hotel in the middle of the night was now a matter for the police. Slim wished the management could have just let him go, but there might be more than he remembered. His memory after going into the bar was fleeting at best. What else might he have done?

On the other side of an industrial estate still under construction, he paused in a lay-by where three large lorries stood parked, their lights off and curtains pulled across their windows, then did his usual checks. No damage to his hands. Nor to his face. Everything of value was on his person, and there were no calls on his phone for which he couldn't recall a reason.

Safe ... or was he?

What else, in his drunken idiocy, might he have done he could no longer remember?

The computer. The sent message.

He needed to know what it had said, what implications it might have. For now, though, he had to keep his head down.

A siren rose in the distance, increased in volume as it approached, then faded as the car roared away in the direction of Plymouth.

If he was really wanted, soon they would get smart and begin a proper search. He made his way to a bus shelter at the end of the lay-by where a single dim solar light illuminated a timetable. He set down his bag, pulled out a sheet of paper, then copied down all the important numbers from his phone's contacts list.

A little farther on, he crossed a small bridge over a brook rushing through rocks in the direction of the River Dart. He lifted the phone, gave the old Nokia a wistful smile, then tossed it into the water.

It was like throwing away an old friend. Slim watched the still-lit display jostling through the water until the light went out, then he shouldered his bag and moved on.

He took a lane heading off the main road as soon as he could. He had studied tracking during his military training and knew he needed to leave no trail. The phone was gone now but if the police really wanted to find him they would trace his route. He doubted he was worthy of a helicopter, but he might warrant a couple of cars if the police had felt it necessary to contact Kim. He kept to the centre of the road, avoiding the verges on either side where he could leave prints. Then, at a suitable gateway, where a wide field sloped down towards the river valley, he pulled off his boots, pushed them into his bag, and continued in his socks.

Shoe prints or even those left by bare feet were easily traceable, but no one ever looked for sock prints, because, frankly, it was the last thing a fugitive considered. It felt oddly satisfying to feel the press of damp earth beneath his feet as he skirted the edge of the field, using the hedgerow as a guide. In the distance, he glimpsed the lights of Dartmouth through the trees, the wide, glittering expanse of the River Dart, and the glow of Kingswear on the opposite hill.

He knew where he needed to go. With muddy socks pushed into a coat pocket and boots back on over his bare feet, he pulled a handful of change from his pocket and caught the first morning ferry from Dartmouth across the river, standing among a huddle of reluctant workers with frosty breath, the chill sea breeze and the salty air working together to keep the exhaustion away. In Kingswear he was too early for the first train, so he followed the railway line in a shambling stumble, keeping his head down, his eyes on his feet while the sky lightened above him and shadows crept back beneath trees and stones.

His investigation called for a dramatic change of angle, one he could not achieve by following the rules. He had always had an opinion of a stubborn case that sometimes it needed to be kicked, broken open, often in a way which might leave him on the wrong side of the law. If you could expose the soft underbelly hidden below the armour, you could go for the kill. It had worked for Slim before, and now, as the sun began to flicker through the trees, bringing with it the day's first warmth, Slim hoped it would work for him again.

The calls of the waking birds provided a pleasant accompaniment as he headed down the forest path near the entrance to Greenway and followed the line of the old railway cutting. Sunlight sparkled off the exposed steel of the collapsed bridge as Slim turned off the path and waded through the undergrowth.

He had drunk a lot. Far more than he had on any recent binge, because even though he was sobering up, he still felt that vacancy the booze brought propelling him forward, pushing him into the very grip of his darkest fears as he stepped over the threshold of the abandoned house and set his bag down.

Whether he had seen movement, whether the fishermen had seen lights, and whether or not any of it was connected to the apparent suicides of Max Carson and Irene Long, it didn't matter. He was here, in the very eye of his fear.

When he woke he would have to face it. For now though, all that mattered was that he was weary beyond words.

With an exhausted sigh, he pushed through a broken door into a back room, cleared weeds and other debris off what remained of an old metal-framed bed, then spread out his coat and lay down.

27

He awoke sometime in the afternoon. The thumping headache initially overruled the fear of waking in an unknown place or of who might now be on his trail, but once he had waded down through the undergrowth outside and taken a drink from the brook pooling behind the dam made by the collapsed bridge, he took better stock of his predicament.

Returning to the house, he now saw it for what it was, just a tumbledown ruin perhaps fifty years empty. Only the barest minimum of glass remained in any of the windows. In the building's centre a wooden staircase that rose to a second floor was partially collapsed, although a second stone staircase on the outer side wall still stood. The downstairs consisted of two large rooms on either side of the entrance, with a kitchen, a utility room, and a small bedroom through a doorway behind the central stairs.

It had the look of a smallholding, and may have stood for some centuries before the construction of Greenway's

Victorian elegance on the hillside above it. While the room to the left had a paved stone floor, the one to the right was dirt, perhaps once used to shelter livestock. The kitchen at the back retained nothing of its former glory besides the rusted remains of an old iron stove and a few piles of sawdust with metal frames emerging from them like the bones of old robots. Slim felt like an archaeologist as he poked through the rooms, looking for evidence of recent habitation or traces of long-gone residents.

He found some, but only what most detectives would consider contamination. A few discarded cans, confectionery wrappers, an empty, faded tobacco packet. The embers of a fire in the corner of one downstairs room. From the subsequent decay of the remaining kindling, Slim estimated it was a year old at least, and therefore unlikely the reason for the lights the fishermen had mentioned. For those he found little other evidence. A couple of heavy boot prints that could have been made by policemen during the recent investigation into Carson's death, but they stopped in the dirt inside the front entrance and went no farther. Otherwise, the only thing that even resembled a print was a couple of muddy splodges on the lower steps of the central staircase, which were fanned out as though made by a large water bird. Slim could imagine a duck, fresh from sifting through the marshland behind the collapsed bridge, taking a couple of steps up before thinking better of it.

Slim used the outside staircase to reach the upper floor. Besides a few loose stones, it had stood the test of time with apparent ease. Here he saw more signs of muck as though animals wading through the marsh had sought out the higher vantage point.

The upstairs floorboards were in surprisingly good condition except in one corner where the roof had partially collapsed and a tree had grown up, branches reaching through holes in the wall as though trying to reclaim it. The rest of the floor was scattered with leaf litter and bird droppings, while through the hole in the roof Slim heard a faint rustle that suggested roosting bats.

Two windows, set low into the wall, offered a view over the inlet and the curve of the River Dart angling off to the south. The collapsed bridge was visible at the end of a tangle of vegetation.

Tree branches overhung the second of the windows, obstructing the view, so Slim knelt down to see better. He lifted a hand and rested it on the stone window ledge, looking down as he found dried mud crusted over the edge.

A small fishing boat was making its way up the river. Slim watched it chug through the water against the tide, the river splashing whitewater against its hull, and wondered if the lights the fishermen had claimed to have seen had come from this very spot.

28

He didn't wait until dark before getting to work. Using skills he had learned during his time in the army, he began to set traps and alarms around the house to warn him of the approach of any strangers. He set his traps in ways that looked natural, trip wires and subtly placed items photographed with his digital camera, the later movement of which would notify him of trespass.

Then, with his location secured, he set about extending his knowledge of his immediate surroundings, moving in a gradual circle through the undergrowth, working his way down as far as the water's edge, then up through the woods, so close to the borders of Greenway's manicured gardens that through the trees he could see tourists moving about. As the shadows lengthened across the lawns and pathways, the evening sun glinting off pale jackets and slacks, they looked like the ghosts he realised he was hunting.

At five p.m. the house closed up for the night, but

with a few hours of midsummer daylight to go, Slim set the second stage of his reconnaissance into action.

He had two requirements for his survival in the pseudo wilderness by the shores of the River Dart. One was a way to continue his investigation, and the other was the more pressing need for sustenance.

Greenway, a sprawling National Trust property complete with a visitor centre and a café set up in an old stables area, had the means to provide both.

Patience. The ability to sit still for hours and simply observe was a military-learned skill Slim had spent twenty years forgetting, but now it was needed, it came back easily. Cameras surrounded the property. Slim crept as close as he could without revealing himself from the undergrowth, then made a mental note of their exact locations and their viewing range.

Those most likely to record his movements were fixed level with the second floor, one with a view of the outer courtyard, one of the approach road, another of the main entrance. However, it would be easy to hide his identity, and it was unlikely there was active security on a historical property. As long as he offered no clear identification and set off no alarms, he could move about without concern.

Slim retreated to his observer's position, again considering the security aspects as a whole, and what would be the easiest way to enter undetected.

Costs had been cut in subtle ways, he soon discovered, after making a circuit of the property from the cover of the gardens. While the building had an alarm system, it only extended through the ground floor and the main windows of the first. With a way up and the right equipment, Slim could easily gain access through one of the narrow hall windows, but at the moment he had no interest in the main building.

The visitor centre was set up in a converted outhouse. Where solid stone walls hadn't been available, prefab plastic and glass had been installed. A camera covered the front entrance, but by climbing over a wall farther along, Slim was able to approach from the unmonitored rear.

A single camera attached to a corner of the house covered the visitor centre and rear gardens, but a line of hedge gave enough cover for Slim to get within a stone's throw of the wall, and a shimmy across a lawn in the dark got him close to the doors.

He had noticed the telltale wires on the front entrance to hint at an alarm, but on the rear there was nothing. Hidden by shadows, Slim pulled what looked like a small plastic spatula from his coat pocket and used it to pick out the rubber lining surrounding a side window about fifty centimetres by thirty. With a piece of cloth he lifted out a single pane of glass, left it propped against the wall then removed his boots and climbed inside.

He had dried out his socks over a window ledge earlier in the day and shaken out the dust. Now they were clean enough to leave no trace of his passing as he climbed inside.

Inside the staff office, the only light came from a sliver of moon across the floor. Slim took out his digital camera and used the display light to collect serial numbers, Wi-Fi codes, and model IDs from the backs of two computers.

Satisfied with his catch, he retreated to his point of

entry and replaced the pane of window glass after climbing out. Careful inspection would reveal what he had done, but he hoped that the volunteer staff were not vigilant enough to notice a loose pane of glass.

Feeling happier than he had in a while, he slipped away into the night.

29

'Don, it's me.'

'Slim! Mate, where are you? How did you get on with that information I set you?'

Slim looked through the dirty glass of the phone box window at a car passing the Sevenoaks Inn and heading across a road bridge into Totnes's eastern suburbs. It was unlikely the phone was being monitored, but discretion was still best. He let Don's questions ride, then said, 'I need some computer gear assessed. Specifically, I need to gain entry to a system, and I need it to be secure and non-traceable.'

'You want to crack their files?'

Slim thought of the National Trust computer, of what hideous secrets it was likely to contain, and smiled.

'No,' he said. 'I just need to use it. I don't have access to a computer right now and I need to get online.'

'What can you give me?'

'I have serial numbers, network identification, that kind of thing.'

Don let out a barely audible sigh. 'That's all? All right, fax it through. I can't promise, but I'll see what I can do.'

'Thanks.'

Slim hung up. Glad the incessant rain gave him a reason to cover his face, he walked along the winding Ticklemore Street and turned on to Victoria Street where he found Totnes public library. There, he faxed Don what information he had, then made up a library card using his fake ID for Mike Lewis, BBC researcher. He checked out a couple of books on local history and headed back out into the rain.

Half an hour later, his conscience getting the better of him, he slipped into a different phone box and called Kim.

'Mr. Hardy! Are you all right? Where have you been?'

'I'm fine, Kim—'

'I must say, Mr. Hardy, that you're really stretching the limits of the people around you with this behaviour—'

'I'm sorry, but I can't explain right now. I just want you to know that I'm fine and not to worry.'

'Well, of course I'm pleased to hear that, but I've had the police on the phone. You walked out of a hotel in the middle of the night after trashing the bar.'

Slim winced. 'I don't remember that.'

'You'll only make things worse if you don't hand yourself in.'

'I can't right now. I have things going on.'

'What things?'

'I can't say. But I'm safe. And I'll be in touch again soon.'

'Mr. Hardy, you're insufferable—'

Slim ended the call. He hung up the receiver with a

sigh then wiped the handset clean of prints with a rag. Adjusting his hood, he headed out.

So, he was wanted for questioning. He had no recollection of trashing the hotel bar, but a charge of public disorder and criminal damage was preferable to being linked to a possible murder.

Concerned he was leaving too wide a trail, he caught a local bus which dropped him off in Paignton.

There, he found another phone box outside the railway station and called another old friend, Ben Holland. Formerly Slim's squad leader during his military days, Ben had left the army and taken up a position in the Metropolitan Police. Calling him was a risk; if there was a warrant out for his arrest, Ben might find himself in a conflict of loyalties. They hadn't been such great friends that Slim could guarantee Ben's discretion.

'Ben, it's Slim. How are you?'

'Slim? John Hardy? God, it's been a while. I'm glad things worked out for you last time.'

Slim remembered the last occasion he had needed Ben's help. He had solved the case but still bore the scars, both physical and mental.

'I appreciate everything you did for me,' he said.

'It was nothing. What are you working on this time?'

'I need details of an ongoing investigation,' he said, then briefly outlined the case. 'I'm afraid I'm getting a little close to a few lines, and I need to find out what's going on. No official information is available.'

Ben sighed. 'As always, you don't ask for much, Slim. I'll make a couple of calls. I have an old friend in Devon and Cornwall Police who might be able to help. How can I get back in touch?'

'I'm afraid I lost my phone, and I can't trust emails right now. I'll call you back in a couple of days.'

'Are you in trouble?'

Slim considered whether to confess his fears to Ben, then decided it might be the foot in the door Ben needed.

'I'm afraid I might be,' he said.

'I see.' A long pause. 'And if I don't hear from you?'

Slim grimaced. 'Then I'm either in prison … or dead.'

30

No change at the abandoned house. No sign of entry at any of the doors or windows. Slim hung his wet clothes over the remains of a stair banister, then climbed to the second floor and sat by the easternmost window from where he had the best view of the collapsed railway bridge and the River Dart's languid flow.

There, sitting naked except for his underwear, he ate some stale bread he had stolen from Greenway's bins, together with a packet of fruit salad he had bought from a Totnes street vendor. After all, he had to keep his balance right, he thought, smiling grimly and wishing he had something which would warm him up a little.

The handful of notes in his wallet would last a few more days at most, even if he were frugal. Using an ATM would add another electronic footprint. From his conversation with Kim, he felt it unlikely the police had tapped his office phone, but if they were really searching for him they might use voice-recognition or keyword software to link him to calls made from multiple locations across south Devon, and his hooded, shuffling image no doubt already appeared on a hundred CCTV cameras. That he was hiding out in the woods barely made him safer; sooner or later they might connect him with Carson's death and come sweeping through.

He needed a clear plan of action because his thoughts and aims were a tangled mess. He had no idea if he was hunting a serial killer or trying to link two unrelated suicides to an attack on his own life. If he could get inside information on the extent of the police investigation, it would give him an idea of where to start his own. As he stared down at the ruined railway bridge, he wondered how quickly he was going insane.

Then something caught his eye, a small motorboat out on the river. As Slim watched, a man stood up in the bow and threw something over the side.

The rain had cleared, replaced by gentle cloud cover. Slim watched the figure feed out a chain then return to the tiny cabin and retrieve something large and square.

An easel. The man appeared to bolt the frame to the boat's floor then pull up a stool and sit down.

Alan McDonald, the elusive painter.

Slim eyed the distance to the boat. It had been a long time since he had intentionally swum anywhere, but the painter would surely notice his approach and flee. In addition, he would be fighting against the river current. Easy to misjudge the distance, and get pulled downriver long before he reached the boat. It frustrated Slim that the man who might have some answers was so close, but he could do nothing about it. Instead he simply watched the painter for a while as he gently worked on the canvas with a brush. At this distance it was impossible to see what Alan McDonald was painting, but from the angle of the man's position it was likely a downriver view of the Dart or a painting of a local car ferry port across the river from Greenway.

With one eye on the painter, Slim reread the information from Don, searching for an elusive clue that might lead to a chain of others. Nothing. A group of normal people with problems, fears, and family connections, but nothing which obviously set them apart from anyone else. Nothing which hinted at involvement in a terrible crime.

Frustrated, he pulled a pen from his bag and turned over a piece of paper. On the back he began to scribble down dates and times. The day Max Carson had disappeared. Slim, allegedly the last person to see him alive, had been drinking with him on the hotel's terrace at five p.m. While the ferries ran until late, the last train from Kingswear left at six-forty and there were no commuter buses at that time. How realistic was it that Carson had made it to Greenway by public transport?

He would have had to head straight there, yet his demeanour and attitude had suggested a casualness which made such haste unlikely. Had he decided to head there later in the evening, he would have had to arrange his own way across the river.

His body had been discovered at around seven a.m. by a dog walker, and the police claimed that Carson had been dead only a couple of hours by that time.

Carson had made his way there sometime during the night, but for a radio DJ in his sixties with no obvious maritime knowledge or skill, the river might as well have been a hundred-foot glass wall. Carson couldn't have crossed it alone.

Which meant someone had taken him, either willingly or by force.

Slim stood up. As he headed down the outer steps, he glanced up at the sky. Grey clouds were gathering again, threatening rain. Out on the water, the little motorboat had gone.

Slim hoped it would be back.

31

Holed up in the abandoned house, Slim was a rat waiting to be trapped, but combing the narrow streets of Kingswear and Dartmouth he could make himself as elusive as a ghost. Slim Hardy would leave a trail, but as Mike Lewis, BBC researcher, he hoped to lay an alternative which might throw off any pursuers.

He headed first for the cross-river ferry. It was still fifteen minutes before the next crossing and he spotted the ferry master standing on the pier wearing a staff t-shirt and smoking a cigarette.

He introduced himself then pulled a couple of pictures from his pocket, one of Max Carson and another of Irene Long.

The ferry master nodded immediately. 'You're not with the police, are you? Already had them round asking the same question.' He shook his head. 'Yeah, I was on duty both nights, but no, I didn't see them. 'Twas dark, though, and we get a lot of commuters between five and seven. Boat's packed most trips. Could easily have slipped past. What I'm saying is, they didn't stand out.'

'Is there CCTV footage?'

The ferry master nodded. 'Was some outside the marina on the other side. Police took it. No one came back so one could guess it was a blank.'

Slim thanked the ferry master, then took the next ferry across to Dartmouth, keeping one eye on the master in the cabin at the ferry's bow, wondering whether his questions might have aroused suspicion. The man, though, neither glanced back at him nor made any phone calls, so Slim climbed off the ferry on the Dartmouth side with a renewed sense of optimism.

He headed first for the harbour master's office in a building across the street from the pier. He requested tide information, and then asked if any boats had been reported stolen in the last few weeks. One had, later found drifting in the middle of the estuary with a group of drunk tourists onboard. The boat Irene had been found in had, of course, never been set adrift.

There were no reports of others, and in Dartmouth Harbour, Slim was told, river traffic was tightly controlled and monitored, with permits and fees required for most vessels. Had Carson crossed the river on the night of his death, it had to have been beneath the official radar. Glancing up the street into the tourist areas, Slim saw a number of CCTV cameras which might have picked up Carson's passing, but any relevant footage would now be in the hands of the police.

He headed back across the river, hiding among a throng of commuters. There, despite having enough money to take the train, he decided to keep a low profile and walked the three miles back to Greenway.

It was long past regular closing hours but parked cars were backing up the road from the entrance gates. Moving cautiously onwards, Slim passed a signboard announcing a private wedding. Morbidly curious, he stepped off the path, cut through the undergrowth and made his way around the back of the manor house until a view of a garden party appeared through branches buffeted by a light breeze.

He had missed the main ceremony, but the newly wedded couple now sat on a table at the end of the garden, surrounded by circular tables hosting six guests each. An older man held a microphone and was delivering an emotional speech about how much his daughter meant to him while the onlookers expressed their appreciation with a series of sighs, cheers, and claps. Attendants moved among the tables, carrying drinks and collecting dishes.

His curiosity satisfied, Slim was about to return to the abandoned house when a girl emerged from behind the manor house carrying a platter laden with bread rolls. She walked awkwardly, her steps short, her knees close together, as though the load were too heavy for her slender frame and narrow shoulders. Her hair was tied up, perhaps shorter or to disguise its length, but as she turned her head and gave an irritated scowl up at the sun, Slim's breath caught in his throat.

It was her.

Eloise.

32

The garden party had been cleared away and the lawn sat in silence beneath a moon peering through thin clouds as Slim returned to the staff office. No one had yet discovered the window with its loose pane of glass and within minutes Slim was inside.

Using a small torch he covered with a cloth to dim the glare, he located the manager's desk and squatted down beside the chair to inspect the drawers.

Locked.

Slim reached into his pocket for something he could use to pick it, then paused. A slight bulge on the mouse mat beside the computer aroused his curiosity. He lifted the corner, revealing a filing cabinet key lying beneath. With a smile, he memorised the key's exact location then used it to open the largest drawer.

An information folder lay on the top of a pile of other papers and files, lying crooked because of a half-finished jar of instant coffee with a sticker labelling it as "Ray's—

please ask". Slim gave a wistful smile at the thought of a decent cup as he lifted out the file.

Most of the information was general stuff regarding procedures, opening hours, and supplier lists, but near the back Slim found the staff manifests. Conveniently, each member of staff had a small ID picture next to their information. On the last page, listed under "kitchen staff" he found a picture of Eloise. Glum and unsmiling, she had refused to look at the camera, her head slightly tilted downwards to leave shadows over her face. To his surprise, he found her listed as Lauren Trebuchet. More important than an alias, however, were a home address and a phone number.

Slim stared. She lived in Paignton, just a few short miles up the road.

33

What might Eloise—or Lauren, as she was calling herself—be doing working a part-time job at Greenway?

Despite his dwindling resources, Paignton was not so far he couldn't afford the bus fare, even if public transport made him nervous. He headed there the next morning, after a cold and fitful sleep on the upper floor of the abandoned house. Near the bus station, he located an isolated phone box and called Don.

'Slim? Is that you? You don't sound too good.'

After a couple of nights sleeping rough, Slim had picked up a cold, but he shrugged it off.

'I'm fine,' he said. 'Did you have any luck with that computer?'

'I did. It wasn't hard to crack. I managed to break into it using the IP address, then used a nifty little program to view a remembered password. Got a pen? Though you probably won't need it. Agatha. Capital A. Not the most inventive. However, it's not quite as simple as that. I couldn't log in without the user ID. You'll need to find who uses that computer and what their log-in ID is. I imagine it'll be a staff number, something like that.'

'Right.'

'Now, I'm not going to ask what you're doing, because, believe it or not, I actually trust you. However, once you're in, be careful. Clean up after yourself. Delete your browser history, that kind of thing. It won't stop a forensics team, but you don't want a casual user noticing anything amiss. At the very least they'll change their password and put us right back to the start.'

'I understand. Thanks, Don.'

'Take care, Slim.'

Slim hung up. Next he called Ben Holland, but got no answer. He decided against leaving a message for fear of being traced.

Eloise's address was for a block of flats not far from Paignton Station, but there was no convenient place from which her fourth-floor flat could be observed. Slim had no option but to confront her, so he headed upstairs and knocked on her door.

No answer.

He tried again, calling out her name but addressing her as Lauren. He was about to try one last time when a door opened a little way along and an elderly woman leaned out.

'Can you give it a rest?'

'I'm sorry. Are you Lauren Trebuchet's neighbour? Do you know when she'll be back?'

'Yes, and no, I don't. She's never back 'til late most nights. Nine, ten o'clock. Now buzz off or I'll call the police.'

'I'm sorry. I'm leaving now.'

The Angler's Tale

The woman went back inside and slammed her door. Slim had hoped he might ask a few questions, but the rattle of a chain slipping back into place was followed by an increase in the TV's volume.

Back on the street, he found another phone box and tried Ben once more, but again received no answer. With his frustration growing, his cold bringing his mood down, and his frugal spending limiting his dinner to an out-of-date bread roll from the reduced basket of a bakery about to close, he headed back to the bus station.

Through the glass façade, two police officers were visible ambling up and down the open waiting area, seemingly in no hurry to be anywhere. It might have been nothing more than a general patrol, but Slim was spooked enough to retreat to a small park across the street from where he could keep watch.

Were they on to him, or was it pure coincidence? Deciding it wasn't worth the risk, Slim walked along the bus route to pick up his lift at a quieter stop. He missed the first bus, however, caught between two stops as it trundled past. It had started to rain, and he spent a frustrating forty-five minutes waiting in the gloom before another bus came. This one didn't go all the way to Kingswear and left him with a miserable walk back to Greenway. He had planned to go back inside the tourist centre but even had he possessed the energy, he would have left an obvious trail. Feeling like he'd wasted a day, he made his way back down through the forest in the dark.

The rain had left the undergrowth moist and slippery, and he felt like a drowned mouse by the time he staggered out of the forest onto the last stretch of the old railway cutting, a partially obscured moon providing just enough light to make out outlines and greyscales.

He had spent enough time exploring the surrounds that he could find the safest approach to the house in the dark, but the rain had shifted the playing pieces, and halfway to the house's looming angular silhouette he slipped in a patch of wet mud where yesterday grass had been. He caught himself as he fell, but a cough which had been building chose that moment to expel itself, echoing up the valley like a dog's sudden bark.

Slim snapped his mouth shut, covering it instinctively with a muddy hand. The wind sighed. The leaves of the nearest trees rustled, and the undergrowth popped and crackled as something farther upslope began to move.

Something large passed within a couple of steps of where he lay crouched on all fours in the undergrowth. Whatever it was continued on downslope, moving deliberately but without alarm nor haste, as though attempting to avoid the very fall he had made to disturb it. As the seconds ticked past, the sound of its movement grew faint, and the very fear which had held Slim in place loosened its grip. Slowly he rose to his feet.

He turned to look at the river in time to see a figure step out of the undergrowth and onto the old railway cutting. It reached the remains of the steel bridge, increasing its speed now it had surer ground underfoot. It ran to the end and, with a sudden jerk, lifted arms into the air and dived over the edge.

34

The passage of time, a poor mood, and worse health were enough to leave Slim doubtful of every aspect of what he thought he had seen.

He might have seen nothing at all. Or he might have seen the lithe figure of a young woman leaping off the end of the ruined bridge, as naked as the day she was born.

Rationality shone through his fear, that no matter where she might have been, she was gone, and unlikely to return. Even so, Slim, forced to stay in the abandoned house by returning rain and a lack of alternatives, couldn't bear the thought of sleep. Crouched in an alcove beneath the remains of the internal stairs, he attempted to channel memories of his longest nights on patrol during the first Gulf War, trying to stay alert for the slightest sound which might constitute a threat. He failed, opening his eyes to the grey dawn, his body aching and soaked.

A fit of coughing ruined any hope he had for stealth

as he crawled out of his hiding place, but there was no movement besides the fluttering of a couple of birds on the upper floor. Moving slowly, he searched for signs of tracks or other disturbances, but the only boot prints were his own. Rain had come in through the roof, soaking the stairs and leaving puddles on the floor, but while he found animal tracks that might have been a fox, there was no sign of anything human.

Outside, the heavy rain had similarly made signs of passage impossible to ascertain, springing many of his carefully laid traps, so Slim headed straight for the railway cutting and the collapsed bridge.

It was too much to hope to find a body lying broken and bloodied on the rusted bridge remains. Slim climbed down to the marshy ground below and stepped out across the fallen girders, searching for any clues that someone might have been hurt and attempting to flee. He found nothing, no scraps of clothing, no spots of blood, no ragged gashes in the undergrowth where hands or feet had torn their way through.

Standing precariously on partially submerged girders, he shook his head and then started back. He was missing something obvious. Clambering back up onto the walkway, he realised what it was as he twisted to see the wide, languid river flowing past, a little choppier than usual because of the rain. It sucked and pulled at the bank beneath his feet, where concrete buffers had been placed to protect the railway line. They dropped sharply into the water, protruding just a few feet out from the bank. He squatted down to peer at a patch of dried mud on the corner angle of one concrete triangle, too far from the bank to have been caused by splashing water and too high to be the result of tides. And while it had begun to run a little, had it been there during the afternoon yesterday, by now the rain would have washed it away.

He had misjudged his angles. Instead of diving over the edge onto the girders hidden in weeds, his mysterious visitor had stepped nimbly out onto to the concrete buttress protecting the railway cutting, paused long enough to set herself and for a lump of mud caught between her toes to slide down onto the rock, and then pushed off, diving into the deep waters below.

He reached into an inside pocket of his jacket and pulled out a small ziplock bag. Using a flat piece of gravel, he scraped the mud off the rock and put it into the bag, sealing it shut. If the girl had been naked, it might contain some skin cells. If Eloise had a criminal record as she claimed, her DNA would be in a police database.

He sat back on the gravel, gazing out at the water. It had surely been her. Who else could it have been? But why? And how had she known he was here?

It made sense, though. If she wasn't at her home in Paignton, she could have been here at Greenway.

He climbed to his feet, an idea coming to mind.

As he began a trudge up to the house which was becoming more arduous as the days passed and his cold grew worse, he wondered where she might have gone after jumping in the water, and why it appeared, from the lack of any items left behind, that when he had disturbed her, she had already been naked.

35

'Slim? Is that you? Even by your standards, you sound terrible.'

Slim rolled his eyes at Kay Skelton's words, then tried not to stare hungrily at the shop window of an expensive Kingswear bakery across the street. Had anyone else but his old friend said it, Slim would have shrugged it off, but Kay was more astute than most.

'Thanks. Trying to shake a cold.'

'Well, get well soon. What can I help you with?'

'I need a soil sample analysed for human DNA.'

'Slim, I'm a forensic linguist. I don't deal with DNA.'

'Do you know someone who might? This could be important for a case I'm working on. Kay, are you still there?'

The line went quiet for a few seconds, then Slim heard a rustling like a shuffle of papers. 'I might be able to pull in an old favour,' Kay said at last. 'What is it you have?'

The Angler's Tale

'A soil sample that might have been on someone's foot. I need to know who that foot belonged to.'

'Okay. I'll see what I can arrange.'

Kay gave Slim details of where to send the sample, then ended the call. Slim next tried to call Ben Holland, but again got no answer.

Aware that his increasingly ragged appearance was making him stand out among the patrons of Kingswear's well-to-do streets, he caught a bus to Totnes in order to follow up an older, neglected lead.

Terrance Winters' bait and tackle shop stood at the end of a narrow cul-de-sac otherwise made up of craft and art supplies shops. Slim wasn't sure what he planned to say as he pushed through the door, but the presence of an unlikely painting on the wall gave him an ideal opening.

Terrance was seated behind the counter, winding a spool of line while glancing at a newspaper propped open on a stool beside him. Slim nodded hello and then browsed the aisles, feeling a tingle of nerves. The fly fisherman who had taken Slim's party on a trip had never faded from suspicion after Slim had caught someone following him to the lookout point, but as Slim plucked up the nerve to approach the counter, he saw Winters lift an asthma inhaler and take a long draw. Slim gave an inward sigh. Another dead end.

'Anything I can help you with?' Terrance asked as he put the wound spool aside.

'Actually, I was after information,' Slim said, reaching into his pocket and pulling out his fake ID, trusting his luck that Terrance wouldn't remember him from the fishing trip.

'BBC?' Terrance said, raising an eyebrow as he inspected the card.

'Not as glamorous as people always think,' Slim said, offering a conspiratorial smile. 'Not when you're employed to do the grunt work. I spend most of my days walking the streets, knocking on doors. There's only so much coffee they'll let us put on expenses.'

They shared a chuckle before Terrance said, 'So what's brought you to my place?'

'I'm researching for a possible documentary on a unique local artist,' Slim said. 'Alan McDonald. I'm just asking around the area to gauge local opinion, but I see you have a picture of his up there on the wall.'

Terrance glanced up at the painting, a look of surprise on his face. 'That old thing ... it's been there for years. Are you really planning to make a documentary about him?'

'We're just in the research stage at the moment. Following up ideas.'

'BBC One?'

Slim had expected this. 'Three,' he said. 'The channel no one watches. But don't tell anyone I said that. And we're not even in the production stage. Only one in ten of these ideas ever make it to the screen. First we need an angle. Then we need enough information to make it worth developing.'

'What do you want to know? Alan stops by for tackle sometimes.'

'I've spoken to a few people farther up the street and they pointed me in your direction.' Slim hoped Terrance wouldn't call him on the bluff. He'd passed a couple of shops and made a note of their staff's general appearance, but if Terrance asked for details his ruse would be exposed.

'Well, I suppose with someone as aloof as Alan I know him as well as anyone.'

'Do you have contact details?'

As he asked the question, Slim pretended to fix his gaze on a particularly fine reel hung up behind the counter. The slight movement of Terrance's hands as he answered told Slim far more than his words.

'I'm afraid he's … well, just a customer. He pays in cash. If you like, I can take a card or something, pass it to him next time he comes in.'

Slim nodded. 'That would be great. Say, is that a Shimano Calcutta reel you've got up there?' Slim said, quoting the first name he remembered from a fishing magazine he had read back at the Castle View Hotel. 'That's a fine reel. I've had my eye on one for a while but I'm not sure it's worth the upgrade. What do you think?'

'You're an angler, are you?'

'Only an amateur. But for more time….'

Terrance's eyes had lit up at the idea of shop talk, and for the next couple of minutes he waxed lyrical about the reel's qualities and shortcomings. He passed Slim the reel, then offered to show him one which had just come in.

'Sure, if you don't mind,' Slim said.

The moment Terrance turned away and headed into a stockroom behind the counter, Slim shifted the reel to his left hand, reached down with his right and twisted around the ledger book lying on the counter. He flicked it open to the most recently used page, his eyes scanning quickly down the list of names. It appeared to be orders for fishing gear, with names and addresses in one column, specifics, prices, and dates in another.

There, dated three days ago, was one for "Alan, 14 Watt. Rd." Ignoring the rest of the information, Slim flopped the book shut and twisted it back around.

Terrance reappeared, carrying a box. Slim feigned interest for a few minutes, then made his excuses and left. Neither man mentioned the card Slim had offered to leave behind.

36

It didn't take long to figure out that the address in Terrance's sales ledger referred to Wattledown Road on the other side of Totnes. Slim walked across town, stopping a couple of times to rest, endure a bout of coughing, and try to shake off the vicious spectre of a common cold made worse by poor sleeping and malnutrition.

The house, one of a terrace on a quiet street, looked normal enough from the outside. Tired of spying, Slim went directly to the front door and knocked. He received no answer. A name over the letter box in the door said Corrine McDonald. Slim bent and pushed the slit open, but an inside box for catching post blocked any view of the house.

He walked to the end of the street, looking for a way around to the house's rear. An alley was blocked with a tall, padlocked fence, complete with a large PRIVATE ACCESS—RESIDENTS ONLY sign and a twirl of barbed wire along the top just for good measure. Each resident would have a key to the padlock. While climbing over wouldn't be difficult, a couple of CCTV cameras high on the walls to either side of the entrance made it clear the residents weren't messing around. Private meant private.

He did another sweep of the street. A similar line of terraced houses faced Corrine McDonald's terrace, leaving no easy place from which to view it, so Slim went back to the front door, pretended to ring the bell, then stood for a moment, observing it.

It looked just like an ordinary door. However, while the space around his feet was scuffed and clear, the front step farther in was marked with dried moss, lichen, and accumulated dust.

Postmen might come to the step, but no one used this door.

Slim made another show of knocking, then returned to the street, quickly walking out of observation distance. The state of the door had made him nervous in a way he hadn't felt in a while. It might make sense that Alan, a solitary, secretive man, might prefer the use of a back entrance, but his mother would be elderly. Would she want to deal with a padlocked gate each day? Perhaps she was bedridden. In which case, wouldn't any home help use the front door?

The longer Slim lingered, the more he risked being noticed by someone who knew the family. He retreated down the street, pausing again in a small, gated park. There was nowhere from where he could observe either entrance to the house without being exposed, but perhaps he could try a different tack. Alan and his mother had to eat. Alan was well established as a boat person, so Slim assumed he would do his grocery shopping on foot. He did a sweep of the local streets, finding a small private mini-mart with enough produce to be convenient yet small enough to appeal to shoppers wary of crowds.

Slim slipped the fake BBC ID around his neck as he headed inside. The day had faded, and it was getting to the point in late afternoon when an old man come in off the river after a long day of painting and angling might be thinking about dinner. Slim made his way to the tills, where just one girl in her late teens, overweight and underdressed, stood looking bored as he approached.

'I'm looking for someone,' Slim said.

'Oh yeah?'

'I'm from the BBC. I'm looking for a painter—'

A sudden fit of coughing overcame him, bending him double. He hacked into his hands, trying to stop but unable as his body spasmed. As he finally got his coughing under control, he stood up, only to find a burly guy in a security guard's uniform bearing down on him. One big hand took Slim's shoulder, another placed itself in the small of his back, and with arms that felt as strong as metal pipes Slim found himself propelled out of the front entrance.

'No offence, mate, but we're a respectable establishment and you're making us look untidy. We'd all appreciate it if you took your trade elsewhere. Tesco Metro on the high street.'

'I'm from the BBC!' Slim shouted, aware as he said it how ridiculous it must sound.

'Aren't we all, mate?' the security guard said, going back inside. 'Run along now, sir, if you don't mind. And if you have a place to stay tonight I'd suggest a bath.'

Slim tried to say something in return, but another fit of coughing overcame him, and by the time he had got it under control the security guard had gone back inside, and he was staring at a poster offering two packets of crisps for the price of one taped to the glass of a closed door.

37

He gave up. Things beyond his control were happening, but for once it had nothing to do with the drink. He caught a Kingswear-bound bus, getting off at an innocuous stop and walking the rest of the way back to Greenway. The property was closed to customers when he arrived, but through the gates staff were visible moving around inside, cleaning up, resetting the house before tomorrow's opening.

Slim melted into the trees but stayed close, using his military knowledge of terrain and camouflage to establish a position from where he could observe. He didn't have to wait long until he saw her, Eloise disguised as Lauren, moving briskly across the gardens, emptying rubbish bins into plastic bags.

Again he was struck by how normal she looked, a wolf in sheep's clothing now shorn and tidied for a job interview. She could almost be a different person to the one who had claimed blood on her hands.

Not far from where Slim crouched, a bin stood

alongside the path. When she approached to empty it, he could grab her and pull her into the bushes in a couple of swift, decisive seconds. He actually took a step forward as she approached before abruptly catching himself. What the hell was he thinking? Had he fallen so low he was willing to abduct a young girl in his search for answers?

He dropped out of sight, watching through the foliage as Eloise leaned over the bin, pulled out a full sack and replaced it with a fresh one. Within seconds his moment was gone as she walked back across the lawn, holding the sack in one hand.

Slim headed down the slope to the old railway cutting and had barely made it before a fit of coughing overcame him. He lowered his head, muffling the sound as best he could. He was still close enough to Greenway that he might be overheard, so he forced himself to keep moving downhill. When he next looked up, however, he realised he had gone the wrong way. A building appeared through the trees. Slim stepped out onto a path and found himself facing the Raleigh Boathouse, which overhung the river. He stumbled inside, his coughing fit thankfully passed, and found a bench with a view of the water.

He wanted just a few minutes to catch his breath, but when he looked up, he found fate staring him in the face.

Alan McDonald's little motorboat sat moored fifty feet out from the bank. The painter sat in the bilges, facing away from Slim, working on an easel that Slim was close enough to see was a partially finished view of downriver.

Close to the bank, where it began to curve, the river flowed quickly. The water level was down too, suggesting the tide was also drawing on it.

The Angler's Tale

The idea was stupid. Yet here was a man Slim had tried repeatedly to track down and failed. He only wanted to talk.

He climbed over a wall and scrambled down to the riverbank before he could talk himself out of it.

By the water, he stripped off his jacket and sweater, leaving only his jeans and a black t-shirt. Despite what many people believed, the army had taught him that it was easier to stay buoyant in water while partially clothed, with clothing also retaining body heat better in cold water. In addition, his dark garments were less visible from the opposite bank or the deck of other river craft than his pale, sun-starved skin.

A fallen tree branch lay half buried in mud, so Slim pulled it free before lowering himself into the water and pulling the branch in front of him. The cold was stunning, but Slim gritted his teeth, concentrating on the boat a little way downriver, and keeping hold of the branch. The mucky foliage made excellent camouflage as he pushed out into the current.

The water took him immediately, spinning him around. He pushed the branch beneath him to create more drag, but the current was strong and too much struggling threatened to take him wide of Alan's boat. He steadied himself just in time as he came alongside the boat, pushing the branch aside at the last moment to use it as a springboard up.

The small motorboat listed high out of the water, leaving Slim no way to get onboard without giving himself away. He grabbed the side rail and hauled himself, sopping wet, out of the water, a clump of muddy foliage still hooked around his leg.

Alan McDonald let out a terrified wail as his boat first tipped one way, then back the other, sending his easel and paint board crashing to the floor. Slim gasped for breath as he struggled to stand up.

'What do you want?' Alan shouted, backing away.

'I just want to talk,' Slim gasped. 'I just want to ask you some questions. Who ... who is—?

Before he could finish, another fit of coughing overcame him. He doubled over, one hand on the side rail, another on his knee. He was aware of the boat spinning, something in his vision right in front of his eyes making no sense at all, then a heavy and hard object slammed down on the back of his shoulders.

'Get off my boat!' Alan shouted, the easel striking Slim again and breaking this time, showering Slim with splinters of plywood. As a weapon it should have been laughable, but the boat was still rocking and its momentum took Slim over the side. He hit the water face first and went under. He had been partway through a cough and now he choked, drawing in freezing liquid, spluttering as he twisted around, legs flailing for purchase where there was none. He felt unconsciousness closing in and he gave one last desperate kick.

Gasping, he broke the surface, his head thumping, vision a momentary blur. He coughed up water, gasping again until this time his lungs filled with air. He pushed his arms wide, steadying himself, his panic slowly easing as he regained control of his senses.

The boat was still close, but upriver, slowly turning away. From behind a tiller Alan McDonald stared at him, a look of shock mixed with anger on his face. He gave a little shake of his head, then bent to start an engine. As the boat straightened, it turned fully side on, holding its position while the engine idled. Slim, struggling in the current, could only stare as it pulled away. In its motion, though, something caught his eye.

Who is the woman in your paintings?

The single question he most wanted Alan to answer, he had never got a chance to finish. But now, from his position in the water, he realised the answer had been in plain sight all this time, there for anyone to see.

He read the name on the boat's stern once more before it turned out of sight.

Eliza Turkin.

38

He had a name, but no strength left to pursue it, and by the time he had stumbled back to the abandoned house he was no longer sure whether the euphoria of gaining the name was better than the loss of a possible lead.

Food was the last thing on his mind, but his aching stomach thought otherwise, and he hungrily devoured a couple of stale bread rolls he had saved from an earlier scavenge. Although they only made his stomach hurt, it was enough to allow him to sleep, curled up by the upper floor windows, his jacket draped over his naked body, the clothes he had soaked while attempting to accost Alan McDonald hanging from the bare beams overhead.

Sleep was anything but comforting. He woke multiple times, often shivering from the cold, sometimes with the lingering recollection of a violent or horrifying dream which featured suffocating water or mud, or the silhouette of a woman, her face backlit with red. Once, the dream was so vivid he thought he was awake, the woman standing above him, shaking her head, muttering, 'What can we do with you?' under her breath as though unaware he could hear. He thought it was Lia or Kim or perhaps even his long dead mother, returned to admonish him one final time, but when he tried to rise, to tell her not to go, she stepped back into the shadows and disappeared.

∽

The sun was shining down on his face when he awoke. He rolled over, remembering he was naked, shivering at the cool breeze through the window space. He reached for his clothes, finding them mostly dry. His body heat would dry out what dampness was left, provided he could summon some. Weaker than he could ever remember feeling, his lungs and chest ached, his throat raw. As he breathed he felt the urge to cough but swallowed it down, afraid that if he began he wouldn't be able to stop.

He pushed himself up, holding on to the beam for support as he slowly turned around.

And stopped, frozen to the spot. Something sat on the floorboards at the very top of the stairs, right where he couldn't miss it. At first he thought it was something living, its luminosity a sign of vitality. Then he realised it was simply a green plastic basket with the sun shining on it.

Slim approached it as he might once have approached a possible bomb, crouching low and moving forward one slow step at a time. Only when he got within a couple of feet did he accept that it was harmless.

It was filled with survival goods: a few individually wrapped bread rolls, some muesli bars, vitamin drinks. With them was a folded note and beside it a clear plastic pill bottle.

Slim nudged the note with his foot, flipping the sheet of paper open.

I can't have you dying on me. Two per day, one in the morning and one at night.

It took a few moments for the sheer shock of what was happening to register.

Someone not only knew he was here, but they were looking out for him.

The woman he had dreamt about had to have been real. He squeezed his eyes shut, wishing he could remember. Tall, he had thought, but that could have been his perspective. Young, maybe, but the harder he tried to remember, the less sure he became.

It was useless. Even now he felt weak to the point of near delirium. He scooped up an energy drink and quickly downed one of the pills, aware it might still take a couple of days to make any difference.

Almost immediately he felt like an idiot. What if it was a drug designed to subdue him? Perhaps everything was a ploy to capture him the same way Carson had been caught, his ankles bound with twine. Slim started to put his fingers into his throat when another image came back to him.

The twine.

He remembered where he had seen it.

In the bottom of Alan McDonald's boat.

39

'Eliza Turkin? Sounds like a character from a book.'

Slim nodded, holding a hand over the phone while he coughed. 'Yes,' he muttered. 'Anything you can find out about someone in the Dartmouth area with that name.'

'Got it. Shouldn't be too hard. Give me a couple of days.'

'Thanks.'

Slim hung off. For a few seconds he leaned on the payphone's metal body, waiting for the dizziness to subside. Despite the medicine, he felt little better. He stared through the glass at the Kingswear street, wondering whether he should have chanced the bus rather than endure the strenuous walk in his condition.

He tried Ben Holland next, but again got no answer. Frustrated, he headed back to Greenway, making it just before dark. The staff had gone and the building was closed up for the night. For the first time in several days the sky was clear and there was no rain around, so Slim made his way onto the grounds and around to the entrance he had made though the side window. Inside the visitor centre, he crouched down by the computer terminal Don had cracked and opened the drawers.

For once, he got lucky. Someone had left an ID card on top of the staff roster folder. Slim withdrew the card from its little plastic jacket and found a computer ID printed on the back.

He switched on the computer and loaded up the log-on screen. He needed the ID to match the password Don had retrieved. He started to sweat as an hourglass appeared, slowly revolving. Slim counted the seconds, but finally it let him inside.

Don had told him to cover his tracks, but Slim had no interest in the National Trust database. He went straight for the internet, loading up his old, underused social media pages.

It had been several days since he had gone pseudo undercover, and this was his first chance to view the email he had drunkenly sent before fleeing the hotel.

He had sent it to Eloise's Facebook account. He first requested that she talk to him, then continued with a rambling paragraph forgiving her for any involvement in his fall from the pier. He closed with another plea for her to get into contact which was so close to begging it made him cringe. The whole message was littered with spelling, grammatical, and word choice errors, leaving it barely legible. Her simple, brief reply, however, was sharp and clear.

I'll kill you for what you did.

Slim frowned. What was he supposed to have done?

He checked her social media page but there were no

comments or updates. Then he checked his own long-neglected page and found that the girl had clumsily posted the same message to his newsfeed. It was a sign of how little time he spent culturing his online presence that none of his few acquaintances had commented.

He checked a few other things, including a brief online search for Eliza Turkin, which, as expected, yielded no results, then came back to the private message.

Did Eloise still feel the same? Was it worth sending a reply? One way or another, he had to talk to her.

He glanced at the message again, noticing the READ time stamp in the corner. If she was still following him, she now knew he had seen the message.

40

STILL FEELING FOUL BUT WITH AN ARTIFICIAL BUOYANCY caused by the energy drinks and food his benefactor had left, Slim vainly set up his traps again before attempting to sleep, but when he woke everything was as he had left it. No one had come in the night this time.

He felt a little better, so he planned to head to Paignton, but by the time he had walked to Greenway Halt Station, his legs were shaking with exhaustion. He had just missed a Paignton-bound train, but one headed for Kingswear was due to arrive in the next couple of minutes.

Craving the warmth and comfort of coffee and heating, he headed instead for the nearer town, then made his way to his favourite quiet café where he pulled out the folder of information Don had sent.

Bringing over a second coffee, the proprietor, a man in his early sixties, asked after his health. Slim glanced down at his clothes, at the stains left by the mud and the river, and the dozen tears and frays from catching on branches and brambles. Perhaps only the folder of notes kept him from appearing homeless.

'I'm feeling a little under the weather,' he told the man, who until now had never openly spoken to him. 'I'm sure it's just a bug.'

'You seem like a nice enough fellow,' the man said. 'If you want to use the back room to clean up a little, I wouldn't mind.'

'Clean up?'

The man looked uncomfortable. 'There's no easy way to say this, but you smell bad and you look worse. I'm concerned about what other customers might think. Like I say, I'm not throwing you out. I can see you're busy, but—'

'I'm looking for a woman called Eliza Turkin,' Slim blurted, cutting the man off. 'I don't suppose that name rings any kind of a bell?'

The man frowned, then gave a little shake of his head. Slim expected a shrug and a blow-off, but then the man said: 'Well, you're a bit late to that party. A hundred years, more like.'

'So you know of her?'

The man shrugged. 'Only the legend.'

'What legend?'

'The one about what they did to her.'

At Slim's incredulous stare, the café owner added, 'Look, get yourself cleaned up and then I'll show you something. I've been wondering what you were doing all this time. I thought you were on the run or something. If I'd known you were a historical researcher I'd have spoken up sooner.'

At no point had Slim claimed to be a historical

researcher, but he saw no reason to correct the man's opinion.

'Sure,' he said. 'I'd like to hear what you have to say.'

~

The proprietor of the café told Slim his name was James Wilson. After a welcome hot shower, Slim found himself sitting in a small living room with a window that overlooked the river and Dartmouth on the other side, wearing a borrowed dressing gown while James ran his clothes through a washer-dryer.

'Why are you being so kind to me?' Slim asked, as James sat down opposite, holding a notebook in his hands.

'Because you were carrying a lot of notes for one small story,' he said. 'It didn't look like you'd found many answers.'

'And you have them?'

James shook his head. 'No, not at all. That woman is more questions than answers. I've heard the other stories. They're not common now, but when I was a boy, we used to make up new ones just to freak each other out.'

'Is there a common one? One which might be true?'

James shrugged. 'I don't know,' he said.

Slim nodded at the book. 'And that's yours?'

James laughed. 'Oh, no. This is just something I used to work on in my free time. A book of local history I never finished. I thought I'd show you what I found out about Eliza Turkin.'

He passed the notebook across to Slim, who began to read.

Eliza Turkin—origins unknown—lived in a cottage on the grounds of Greenway. Employed as a housekeeper by two generations of owners, it was long rumoured that she had a darker side. Thought by many to also be a notorious prostitute in the Dartmouth area known only as Old Bea, accusations against her grew so loud that on the night of December 1st, 1901, a mob dragged her from her home and allegedly murdered her. While no record remains of the method of death employed, the most common rumour is that she had rocks tied to her feet and was thrown into the mud of Wellwater Inlet, which can be thirty feet deep on a spring tide. Rumours persist that Eliza was considered something of a sea witch, and that sending her back to the sea was the only way to break her curse over the area.

Slim looked up. 'What curse?' he asked.

James smiled and shrugged. 'I never have found out,' he said. 'People don't like to talk about her. She's like the Dart Estuary's dirty little secret.'

'You must have some suspicions?'

'Of course. But nothing concrete. Nothing I can prove.'

'Tell me, please.'

'Why such an interest?'

Slim let out a slow breath. 'I'm not a historical researcher, as you assumed,' he said. 'I'm actually a private investigator.' Then, with a shrug, he added, 'I'm also a functioning alcoholic. During a stay on a rehabilitation course in Dartmouth a month ago, two people allegedly committed suicide. I've been investigating their deaths, but more than that, I believe I've come under suspicion from the police. I'm trying to find out what happened to them in order to clear my own name.'

James nodded. 'Well, that makes sense, I suppose. Max Carson and Irene Long, wasn't it?'

'You know of them?'

'Oh, word gets around. People talk and all that. I don't know about Long, but Carson died up there, didn't he? Up by Wellwater Inlet?'

'Yes, he did.'

'He was probably looking for her.'

'What on earth do you mean?'

'Well, kids would go up there sometimes, hunting Old Bea as they called her, even though she and Eliza Turkin were supposedly two different people.'

'I've heard mention of Old Bea. She was a prostitute?'

'Supposedly. Back when the Dart Estuary took more commercial trade, mid-nineteenth century sometime. Old Bea ran a brothel in Dartmouth. The rumour went that she took every sailor herself before passing them off to her girls.'

'A rumour?'

'Of course. One of many. It was believed she got pregnant so often that she was known as the mother of street children. And her rages were apparently so great they'd whip up a storm out to sea. Sailors in the area still talk of Old Bea when a sudden storm hits. Heaven help a sailor who couldn't pay her rates.'

'What happened to her?'

James smiled. 'I imagine she died a prostitute's uneventful death and ended up in an unmarked grave.'

Slim lifted an eyebrow. 'And what does the legend say?'

James laughed. 'Her brothel eventually burned down. Old Bea was likely cast out on the street, but the legend is that she stole a rowing boat and drifted out to sea, where she was claimed by the most vicious of storms.'

'Interesting,' Slim said, rubbing his chin as he remembered the rowing boat containing the body of Irene Long.

'Quite.'

'Yet she and Eliza are often considered one and the same?'

'The legends of two old sea witches tend to blend together, yes.' He smiled. 'Back in those days, people didn't have the internet to fact-check.'

'And do you believe that?'

James shook his head. 'Oh no, not at all.' He had assumed a small smile which gave Slim the impression he had something else he was desperate to share.

'What do you really think? Totally speculatively, of course.'

James leaned forward as though he had been waiting for this moment. 'Well, there are certain facts that fit. Eliza died in 1901; there's a historical record of it—an obituary in a local newspaper. While I've found no historical mention of Old Bea, she's often associated with the mid-nineteenth century. Move her just a couple of decades forward, however, and you find a link.'

'Tell me.'

'In 1885 there is a record of a great fire in Dartmouth, engulfing the Mariner's Arms, a hotel and tavern on the waterfront. The building was gutted, torn down. Eliza Turkin was a woman of no known parentage. She was allegedly an orphan left on the steps of Greenway as a baby and raised by the servants to work in the household. She was around thirty at the time of her death. Old Bea, at the time of hers, was described as a "broad, bawdy matron with arms like trees, and thighs strong enough to crush the most durable of men." That's from a poem dated 1880. Doesn't sound like a young woman, does it?'

Slim shook his head. 'No, it doesn't.'

James had a twinkle in his eye as he said, 'If you assume that Eliza was left at the building that later became Greenway in 1870 or so, and estimate that the woman from the poem was in her forties or fifties, the relationship would fit.'

'What relationship?'

'I think Old Bea was Eliza Turkin's mother.'

41

Slim barely noticed the journey as he walked back to Greenway, lost in thought. James Wilson, despite giving him little practical information, had fired up Slim's imagination.

A notorious local prostitute dead at sea and a woman murdered for being a sea witch, possibly mother and daughter. It was fanciful, fantastical, the sort of novel fodder Slim would have dismissed if it wasn't clear that both Carson and Long had possessed some sort of knowledge of either or both. Carson had died at the spot where Eliza Turkin had both lived and died, while Irene's attempt at a dramatic death couldn't surely have paralleled Old Bea's legendry one by pure coincidence.

At a payphone near Greenway Halt, Slim rang Don to give him an update.

'Eliza Turkin was considered a sea witch,' he said. 'I need to know why and what that means.'

Don laughed. 'Give me another day,' he said.

Next, Slim called Kay. 'Any news on that DNA sample?' he asked.

'I passed it to a friend who ran it and extracted human DNA,' he said. 'You were right, there was someone there.'

'Did you get a match?'

Kay sighed. 'It's not that easy. A DNA record only exists for convicted criminals, and even that's in its infancy. My contact managed to break through the database security and run the sample, but we found no match.'

Slim clenched a fist in frustration. It ruled out Eloise, assuming she had a criminal record like she had claimed. But what if she had been lying? The girl's entire existence had felt like something out of a bad dream.

'If I can get you a sample, could your friend run a test to see if it matched that in the soil?'

'I'm no expert, but I would suppose so,' Kay said.

'Give me a couple of days,' Slim said.

Eloise was working at Greenway, so her DNA would be present somewhere. However, Slim had no way to be sure what exactly she had touched, and whether or not it had been contaminated by other people. He needed a surer sample.

A nearby bus timetable had one last bus heading for Paignton. Slim was exhausted already but unlikely to get a decent sleep in the abandoned house anyway. When the bus pulled in a few minutes later, he climbed aboard, trying to doze with his head leaning on his bunched jacket as it meandered towards its destination.

By the time he had walked the rest of the way to Eloise's flat his legs were shaking and he found himself sitting down on a grass verge as he considered what to do. He could wait, watch for her, identify something she had touched and then wipe it with a rag. The sample might be enough.

Breaking and entering a private property was not something he had ever done lightly, but there were times it had been called for, and over the years Slim had developed a level of expertise. He pulled a small object from his pocket and turned it over in his fingers.

Eloise's door opened with a Yale lock. It had a second lock lower down which would cause greater problems if Eloise had used it, but the small metal device he now held would deal with the Yale with ease. Military-issue, it had been a gift from an old friend.

Slim pulled his hood over his head, gloves over his hands, and stood up. For a few seconds, a wave of dizziness overcame him, and he clung to a wall for support. Despite the medicine his mysterious benefactor had provided, he was still some way short of full health.

As the dizziness cleared, he headed across the road and into the covered stairwell of Eloise's building.

The angle of the moon told him it was nearly eleven p.m. No light came from under Eloise's door and no sound came from inside. If home, she might be sleeping, so Slim eased his pick into the lock and twisted it until he heard a small click. The door gave immediately, indicating the lower lock was unused. This in turn suggested no one was home, so Slim quickly stepped inside and pulled the door closed.

A hall led to a door at the far end. A small kitchen led off through an arch to one side. A window above the sink gave enough light from the moonlit sky outside for Slim to see a tiny shower cubicle through an opposite door.

A small, soft-framed suitcase stood by the bathroom door. Slim nudged it open with his boot. Inside were several folded items of clothing, a couple of women's magazines, and a toiletries bag. The handle of a hairbrush protruded from an unzipped side.

Slim stared. All he needed was a single strand of hair. He nudged the brush handle with his boot, the loose zip opening a little farther to reveal bristles. Slim reached down and pulled out a strand of hair tangled around a few bristles near the handle's base. He slipped it into his jacket pocket and nudged the suitcase's lid closed.

It was enough. He could leave, but his curiosity took hold as he looked up at the closed door.

Instinctively he reached up and tried the hall light, but wasn't surprised to find it didn't work. Already the lack of personal effects and the pile of takeaway boxes on the kitchen counter told him much about Eloise's state of living.

The water might be running but no one had bothered to switch on the electricity. Even so, as Slim reached the door and gently eased it open, he was unprepared for what he might find in the room beyond.

∾

Nothing.

A least, nothing to suggest any form of permanency. A suitcase stood against a wall, a rolled sleeping bag and deflated inflatable pillow lying on top. A few items of clothing, folded, poking out of a plastic bag emblazoned with the logo of a local launderette.

For someone working for the National Trust, Eloise had certainly made little effort to settle in.

As Slim stared at a folded uniform laid neatly over a cardboard box, he felt a sudden jolt of unease. She had been home and gone out again, meaning she could return at any moment. Remembering that he had what he had come for, he retreated to the door.

As he let himself out of the flat, he released a slow breath. Back in control, he headed downstairs. On a corner a street away he found a newsagent still open. He bought an envelope and stamps and mailed the hair sample to Kay. Then, with little else to do now that he was stuck in Paignton overnight, he found a kebab shop with a small seating area and bought a coffee. Sitting in the window with a view of the street, he realised that if Eloise had headed into the town centre she would surely return this way.

However, multiple coffees and a free burger later, 'because you're cleaner than most of them,' the manager announced he was closing up and ushered Slim out into the night.

Nearly three a.m. No sign of Eloise, but Slim was tired of this part of town. Caffeine-loaded to the point that his vision was blurring, he headed for the bus station and the dreamy hope for decent sleep. He dozed on a corner bench while a group of drunks argued at the other end, then climbed aboard the first available bus out of town.

The inlet was quiet, the house still as he climbed the stairs to the second floor. To his frustration, he found his mysterious benefactor had been again, leaving him with some packets of biscuits and sandwiches, as well as, luckily, considering the chills that were racking his aching body, a blanket. His benefactor shopped in Tesco, he discovered, meaning it could be practically anyone.

Aware he could be destroying ways to identify them but not caring, he ripped open a packet and stuffed a tuna sandwich into his mouth, then pulled the blanket over his knees.

As he lifted it, a note fell out on to his lap. He opened the folded piece of generic A4 paper and read a single line:

Don't give up.

'I won't,' he muttered, feeling the dryness at the back of his throat threatening to develop into a burst of coughing. 'But let me get a decent sleep first.'

As he lay down, his thoughts refused to settle. Eloise's face flashed in his mind, a sadistic grin almost mocking him.

Why can't you find me, Slim? I'm right in front of you, haunting you.

42

He woke in late morning with a feeling like he'd been run over by a truck. His cough had returned, and for a few minutes it assaulted him, drawing his back into spasms and his stomach into a tightness he thought would make something snap. When it let him go, he looked around, quickly eating the rest of the food left for him and swallowing a couple more of the pills.

After getting himself into a semblance of order, he hiked up through the woods then did a circuit of Greenway via the most outlying paths. Open for business and with clear skies overhead, the gardens were packed with tourists. Feeling a rare boldness, Slim shed his battered jacket and slipped onto the site, mingling with other tourists as he headed for the house. He wanted a look at Eloise, but aware she would recognise him, he needed to establish her location first.

He approached an elderly staff member standing near the main doors. The man, neatly dressed in a dapper grey suit, gave Slim a brief visual appraisal but to his credit showed no sign of distaste in his expression as he turned to Slim and smiled.

'Can you help me?' Slim asked. 'I'm looking for a Miss Trebuchet. I bumped into her in Dartmouth and she told me she worked here. I just wanted to say hello?'

The man frowned. 'Trebuchet? Oh, you must mean Lauren. She works in the café but I don't think she's in today. Called in sick.'

'Really? Nothing the matter, I hope.'

The man shrugged. 'Sickly little thing. She's always off, so I've heard old Leslie in the café grumbling. Weak constitution.'

Slim forced a chuckle. 'Young people these days.'

'Right.'

'Shall I tell her you stopped by?'

'Ah, sure.'

'Your name?'

Slim hesitated. 'John,' he said at last. 'Tell her John from Dartmouth.'

'John from Dartmouth.' Suspicion had returned to the old man's eyes. 'Well, you have a nice day.'

'Thanks.'

Slim moved off, barely making it to a nearby secluded part of the garden before a fit of coughing overcame him again.

Why hadn't Eloise shown up for work? It could be something as mundane as a hangover, but would a girl living out of a suitcase be out hitting the bars? There had been no sign of anything untoward in the flat—no smell of booze, no drug paraphernalia, nothing except the indication that it was being used solely as a base, somewhere to leave her things while she undertook certain activities elsewhere.

With a moment of clarity Slim realised that her situation mirrored his own. Could it be they were searching for each other? If she had pushed him off the pier, she would surely know by now that he had survived. Perhaps she was looking for another opportunity.

He headed back down through the woods until he emerged on a riverside path with views of the Dart to both north and south. He felt like a man in a glass cage in the middle of a busy train station, screaming for air while people pushed past all around, oblivious to his situation.

He stared out at the water, hoping for some kind of revelation, a sense that he wasn't running in circles on the tail of a series of murderous ghosts, but all he found was yet more mockery, in the form of an old man, sitting in a boat halfway across the river.

Alan McDonald was facing away from him, a new or well-repaired easel set up in the middle of the boat, his brush hand flicking the canvas with gentle strokes.

How can you do it? Slim wondered, gritting his teeth to stop himself screaming out loud. *How can you sit there painting without a care in the world?*

43

Feeling a little stronger after the food had settled, Slim walked along the railway line into Kingswear. Seeing Alan painting with such carefree abandon so soon after Slim had tried to accost him had left Slim with an itching sense of frustration. If the old painter wouldn't talk, Slim would paint his own picture of the man he was trying to meet.

Kingswear's narrow streets were cluttered with trinket shops, cafés, and restaurants, interspersed with other shops selling traditional crafts and local goods. Slim wandered into an art gallery and began looking around. Before long he noticed the shop assistant giving him an undue amount of attention, so to absolve the obvious suspicion his appearance aroused, he waved the man over.

'I'm looking for anything you might have by Alan McDonald,' he said. 'I believe he's local? I'm something of a collector.'

The man, his suspicions tempered by Slim's directness, shrugged.

'There's a couple of prints over there on display,' he said, pointing to the wall. Slim wandered over and examined two generic riverscapes, then shook his head.

'I'm looking specifically for any he might have containing characters,' he said. 'In particular, Old Bea.'

The man, a decade younger than Slim at least, looked confused. 'Old what?'

'A woman.' Remembering how the staff of the gallery in Totnes had tried to hide the painting of Old Bea in the aftermath of Max Carson's death, and realising the man might be just a subordinate, Slim added, 'Do you have anything out in the back?'

'I can take a look for you.'

The man headed for a door behind the counter. Slim followed close behind, not allowing the man enough time to conceal anything. Seemingly unperturbed, however, the man went straight to a bundle in the corner and carried it over.

'These came in yesterday,' he said. 'As you can see, it's not even opened yet.'

'These are from Alan McDonald?'

The man nodded as he reached for a pair of scissors to cut the twine tied around the bundle. Cardboard wedges fell away to reveal a stack of canvas prints over wooden boards.

'These are only prints,' the man said, taking a couple and turning them over, removing the cardboard sheets put over the fronts to protect them. 'If you want originals, you'll have to go to one of the bigger galleries in

Dartmouth or Totnes.' He grinned. 'We're in the selling-junk-to-tourists trade.'

'Let me just take a look,' Slim said, feigning interest in a picture he had already seen of a woman standing on a wooden jetty as he picked a piece of the binding twine off the floor. It was identical to what he had seen in Alan McDonald's boat.

'This comes from the seller?'

The man looked up. 'Huh? What? Oh, that? It's just baler twine. The artist gets these prints done himself and sends them in. Just a bit of string really. Standard stuff you can buy anywhere.'

Slim forced a laugh. 'I grew up on a farm,' he said. 'Takes me back.'

'It's the small things that do it, eh.'

'Right.'

An awkward moment passed between them before Slim thanked the man and said he'd be on his way. He slipped a thread of the twine he had picked off the tabletop into his pocket on his way out, wondering if it was something significant, or nothing at all.

44

Kay was still waiting to hear from his contact, but Don had some more information.

'I got in touch with a local historian,' he said. 'I've found nothing so far on Old Bea, but I heard another rumour about Eliza Turkin. It was claimed that once old enough to work around the house she gradually elevated her position to head housekeeper. She was never popular among the other servants, however, after attracting the eye of the young master of the house. She allegedly fell pregnant, but to hide the father's identity, rumours were spread that she worked as a prostitute, selling herself to passing sailors from the jetty below her cottage.'

'Fanciful,' Slim said. 'No reason why she would with a regular income.'

'That was what I thought. More likely she had a lover she met in secret.'

'And that was all?'

'No. It was claimed she was seen swimming out to the passing boats, "far faster than could be possible of a pregnant serving woman." That's a direct quote from an old diary my contact owned.'

'The origin of the sea witch rumour?'

'I believe so, but there's more. It was claimed that several children born around Dartmouth suffered similar deformities which were blamed on their parents coming into contact with Eliza. Deformities which could connect them with magic supposedly born from the sea.' Don laughed. 'I mean, this is all fairy tale stuff, Slim. I don't know how much of it'll be of use to you.'

Slim was quiet for a moment. 'Probably not much of it, to be honest, but you never know. What kind of deformity?'

'I could find nothing specific.'

'Any names of these supposed victims?'

'Nothing, but I'll keep looking.'

Slim thanked him and hung up. Frustrated, he resumed his trawl of Kingswear's art galleries, hunting for some kind of clue. Several had no Alan McDonald prints at all, but in the last place he tried—a bric-a-brac store near the harbour—the elderly owner seemed only too pleased to dig out a dusty painting from a back shelf. A price ticket of £100 was so faded Slim could barely read it, and until the man blew the dust off the front to reveal a vivid river view, he had thought the painting equally faded.

'Been sitting there for years,' the old man said. 'Used to try and palm it off on people but never could. Didn't like the look of it.'

Painted from a viewpoint looking upriver towards the jutting hill of Greenway, the river curved left then back right. Eliza Turkin's house was visible in the right-middle, and Slim felt a tingle of unease trickle down his spine.

'Pretty, ain't it?'

'Very. I'm surprised you couldn't find a buyer.'

'Too spooky,' the man said. 'First, it's of an evening, and it's got those two down there in the water.'

Slim frowned. The dust had made the darkened sky difficult to notice, but now he did, he saw how the lines of sky were emphasised against the background hills. And the "two" the old man mentioned were little more than a pair of spots of black against the water's blends of whites, greys, and blues.

'Gotta look from afar,' the old man said. 'Up close ye won't see much.'

He held the painting back a couple of feet. As the brush strokes blurred, they took on the appearance of two figures bobbing in the water.

'They're a bit far out from the bank,' Slim said. 'And there are no boats nearby.'

'That's what puts people off,' the old man said. 'Looks like they's drowning, don't it?'

'It does,' Slim agreed. He chuckled. 'But they're not, are they? That's Eliza Turkin ... and her mother.'

'Beatrice Winter,' the old man said, nodding. 'Figured you was a local lad.'

Slim hid his surprise at the man's revelation. 'Grew up outside Totnes,' he said, hoping his slight northern accent wasn't prominent enough to give him away. 'Always preferred things farther south. Prettier, more history.'

'You a collector?'

'More of a researcher. Thinking of a book. Life and

times of the common people. The sailors, brewers, farmers, that kind of thing.'

'And the downtrodden?'

Slim chuckled again. 'Couldn't leave them out. Not when there were so many.'

'Travesty what happened to her,' the old man said. 'I heard the story, passed down. Watered down, most like, too.'

'Like the beer in Totnes,' Slim said, the joke provoking a cackle from the old man. 'I heard Eliza was a witch.'

'Nothing of the kind, but they blamed her anyhow. Me grandfather was a lad the day they went for her.'

Slim felt as though someone had slapped him across the cheeks. 'He was involved?'

'Told me when he was out of it one time, back when I was working out on the boats. Said he was just an oarsman, rowed the others upriver, waited 'til it was done. Heard the talk though, what they did to her.'

Slim nodded along, trying not to look too keen to hear what the man had to say. 'What they did?'

'Grandfather, he wasn't one to run his mouth, not 'til he'd been on the rum. We were coming back from Totnes after unloading some lobster pots up there. Must be back in the fifties, this. Can't have been more than twelve. He had a few jars off the pier up there and we're passing the inlet on the way back and he says, "She's still down there, lad. Still down there, and if you look too close she'll reach up and pull you down with her."'

'Eliza?'

'Yeah, down there in that muck by the inlet. Her mother got away, see? Set herself free in the open ocean so her bitter spirit could exercise its wrath. Weren't about to let Eliza join her, were they, else the curse would come back.'

'What curse?'

The old man leaned forward, lowering his voice as though not wanting to be overheard. 'Kids born with no hands or feet, but with fins like a fish.'

45

Slim felt too unnerved to return to the abandoned cottage, so headed back to the harbour and took a ferry over to Dartmouth. His mind was racing with ideas, few of which made any sense. Long dead prostitutes, children with fins, women drowned in river mud ... it was enough to keep him from sleep for the next couple of years.

As he got off the ferry and wandered into the backstreets behind Dartmouth's riverside, he felt another darkness closing in even as night fell around him. His cough had held off most of the day, the antibiotics perhaps finally taking effect, but an old longing had returned, the urge to drown himself, to slam a door shut on the horrors of the world and embrace a descent from which he might never return.

It was at these moments that he hated himself the most. Walking through the door of a bar and revelling in the familiarity of the sights and smells, knowing that there would be no mistake, that he had made a conscious decision to be here, that he had chosen a stool of his own free will, waved over the barman and ordered a seemingly innocent glass of liquid which was the gateway to everything that was hellish in his life, and knowing, with complete certainty, that he was choosing to lift it to his lips, to take the first sip on what would be a downward spiral that could only ever end with a crash into a hard, bruising floor.

As always, he began with coherency. Like any good drunk he was the life and soul, a laugh and an ease of manner to gravitate towards. But, like any good drunk, soon there was a moment when things changed, when he had crossed a line and words and thoughts rolled over each other, and a face not smiling was kicking over a stool and moving forwards with fists squeezed into hammers at his sides. And Slim was remembering hard nights in the military when tensions flared and tempers overflowed, and how he'd learned to ward off such troubles only through experience, and how he was now standing up to meet the challenge of the wrong word, the badly timed look. He was aware of pain in his face and his hands, of flashing lights, of doors opening and closing and finally cold gusts of air on his skin and the chill of cobblestones under aching hands.

More hands, flashing lights, a soft seat beneath him, a slamming door. A harsh voice ordering him to sleep it off.

∽

'Wake up.'

A hand struck the side of his face. Slim groaned.

'Come on, get out of here before someone sees me.'

Slim opened his eyes. Still drunk but with the

grogginess of not nearly enough sleep, he tried to focus on the speaker.

He could see nothing other than a silhouette, but the voice belonged to a woman.

'I'm risking everything doing this, you stupid bastard. Get out of here and get moving before we're seen.'

'Huh?'

'You're lucky it was me and not someone else. I'm not sure what you were doing, but I'd keep away from the docks for a while. Fishermen tend to settle things amongst themselves.'

'I don't know—'

'Come on, get out.'

A door opened. Strong hands pushed Slim towards the cold. A grass verge cushioned him as he fell. He managed to push himself into a sitting position long enough to watch the taillights of the car as it sped away, then he slumped back down, wishing the ground would swallow him, wishing he were dead.

∽

Back in the military, Slim could have gone toe-to-toe with most and come out on top, often fuelled by a rage inspired by an unfulfilled childhood, but now, twenty years on, his stomach was smaller than his mouth and the desert-trained physique was a memory. From the look of his hands and the ache when he tried to clench his fists, he had relived his glory days for a while. The numbness at the side of his jaw, the puffiness of his right eye and a loose molar said he'd eventually come out second best.

His actual memory of the night before was a blur to be picked through over time. At least without a phone the aftermath was limited to his immediate vicinity, but what few snippets he recalled of the storm he had unleashed involved men far bigger than him, stools kicking over, a woman screaming in his face. He had a vague recollection of asking about prostitutes, perhaps catching the eye of someone's wife at exactly the wrong time. And as things did, it had escalated from there.

As he lay on his back on the upper floor of Eliza Turkin's old abode, unsure how he had managed the trek through the forest, he felt the same shame and regret that he always did after a relapse. What damage had he done this time? How many people had he hurt?

He tried to push the darkest thoughts from his mind, concentrating instead on how he had got back, trying to remember. The car that had dropped him on the verge outside Greenway.

A woman's voice.

It took him some time to get himself into a workable condition. He had no food left and vomited up the last remaining energy drink right after downing it. Staggering to the river and climbing awkwardly down over the concrete buttresses, he drank as much cold, grainy water as he could stand, then dunked his head into it until he began to feel better.

He climbed back up and sat down on the edge of the abandoned railway cutting, staring at the collapsed bridge. Was Eliza buried somewhere in the mud under there? Had she reached up and dragged Max Carson down?

It was a ridiculous thought. Slim blamed the cold

water for making him shiver, then stuffed his hands into his jacket pockets to warm them.

In his left pocket, his fingers closed over something. He pulled out a beer mat, wincing at the smell of stale beer as he turned it over.

On the underside, someone had written a phone number in bright red pen.

46

Greenway was closed for the day. Slim, after spending some time observing the grounds for staff still on duty, finally made his way inside the complex, first picking a lock on the cafe's door and pilfering a couple of sandwiches, then making his way to the visitor centre.

He felt too sick and weary to hide himself from the video cameras, figuring that they would only be checked if he tripped an alarm. He headed straight for the computer he had cracked, logged onto his social media and checked for any messages.

Nothing. He scanned Eloise's page, but she hadn't been online according to the system since the day she had sent the message.

More out of an unconscious effort to avoid doing anything important, he also checked the social pages of the other main players, finding them as inactive as he had expected. On Irene's, however, someone perhaps unaware of her death had posted a generic picture of a dog and added a comment: *thinking of you today. Hope you're doing ok x.* Slim made a mental note to have Don check the date, although guessing by the picture, it was likely the anniversary of the passing of a beloved pet.

Finally, finding nothing which could help him, he cleared out his viewing history and logged off. Then, aware there was nothing else he could use as an excuse, he pulled out the beer mat and went outside to use a payphone he had seen in the courtyard.

His hands shook as he held the receiver, partly from the hold the booze had regained over him, partly from nerves. He had no recollection of getting the phone number or what it signified. It could be anything at all.

It rang and rang, finally cutting to an automated voicemail which claimed the mailbox was full. Slim let out a held breath. So much for that. At least it was a working number. He grimaced, trying to remember what it was for, but his memories of last night went no further than the fists swinging for his face.

He called Don, passing on the information he had found on Irene's social media page. Don had no other news however, so next he rang Kay.

'Slim, damn it, can't you get a phone so I can contact you?'

'It's a work-in-progress,' Slim answered. 'I'm still off the grid.'

'I've noticed. Look—'

'Kay, someone picked me up yesterday. I don't know who. A woman. Maybe she—'

'Slim, listen to me, will you?'

Slim rubbed his eyes with fingers which ached just a little less than his head. He wondered if total disintegration would make him feel better.

'Don, I—'

'This is Kay, you damn idiot. Just shut up a minute. We found something.'

Slim opened his eyes. He stared at the ground, at boot marks in the gravel, thinking of a different kind of gravel, that of the Iraqi desert.

Where the horrors had first begun.

'Slim? Are you still there?'

He snapped back to reality. 'I'm here. Sorry. Go on.'

'We found a match. My contact ran it through a sex crimes DNA database, and came up with a match.'

'A match?'

'The DNA from the hair sample you sent me. It matched that of a registered sex offender.'

Slim frowned. 'I'm not following. Eloise is a sex offender?'

'Not Eloise, but her DNA sample, it was a fifty-percent match to one on record, meaning it's almost certainly a close member of family.'

'Run that by me again.'

'The original sample relates to a sexual assault charge filed in 2001. It never went to trial because the claimant received a settlement, but the sample given by the accused was kept on record.'

'Who was it?'

Kay took a deep breath. 'Are you sitting down? It was Max Carson.'

47

Eloise Trebuchet was Max Carson's daughter.

It explained a lot.

Heading back to the National Trust visitor centre and logging on to the computer again, Slim did some research of his own to fill in a few of the blanks Kay had left him. Tabloid rumours had peaked for Max Carson in the mid-nineties, when he had briefly crossed from radio over into television to present a couple of late night magazine shows aimed at teenagers and students. Archived articles talked of backstage drug use, affairs with guests, drunken orgies. Slim, who had lived through the tabloid storm of the first Iraq war and had very different memories of it to those he had read about, doubted most of it was true. It was media fodder, one beer turned into twenty, a stolen drunken kiss turned into a months-long affair, a single line of cocaine become a powder storm vacuumed off a prostitute's back.

Where there was water there were usually waves, however, and Eloise's age made it likely she was a product of Max Carson's heyday, before falling ratings and unwanted media attention sent him back to pasture on regional radio.

Among the sludge there were multiple rumours of illegitimate children which would take months to sort through and follow up. What was certain, though, was that Eloise not only had a reason for being in Dartmouth at the time of Carson's death, but had a very real motive for murder.

The rich, famous father who had rejected her. It made perfect sense.

But what about her possible attempt on Slim's life, and the email?

I'll kill you for what you did.

They had been together when the police took Slim for questioning. Did Eloise think Slim was an informant of some kind who had ratted on her?

He cleaned up the computer and headed back outside, feeling a renewed sense of optimism. At last he had a lead. He also had a motive. An illegitimate child spurned by her celebrity father driven to kill him out of revenge. It was worthy of a tabloid spot of its own.

Then why was Eloise still here, working not so secretly in the very place where she could have murdered her father?

Slim grimaced. Only one way to find out.

48

He took a bus to Paignton. With Greenway closed, Eloise had to come home at some point. Nervous about confronting her again, Slim headed straight for her flat, wanting to get it over with. He still felt terrible, the cough shuddering through his body at regular intervals and bringing wary looks from passers-by. With his battered face, unkempt beard and filthy clothes, he imagined he resembled something of a social nightmare. At one point he noticed a road sweeper moving slowly along the street ahead, and wondered if it wouldn't be for the best to just stand and let its spinning brushes drag him away.

No one answered his knock, so he tried again. Silence.

He could retreat to the same kebab shop as before and watch the road, but he might miss her again. His legs ached and all he wanted to do was rest.

He took the pick from his pocket and opened the door.

As he went inside, he reminded himself that Eloise

had possibly tried to kill him. Without doubt she had threatened to do so. He had to be careful.

In the back room he found a place out of her line of sight to crouch as she came through the door. He might need to grab her, and the few seconds' grace before she saw him would prove vital.

He lowered himself down. Her suitcases stood to his right, half in front of him, one lying with its top unsecured, a bundle of garments hanging out.

And something else ... a piece of paper, a photograph—

The front door banged. Slim was so transfixed by the image half protruding from her luggage that he was left motionless as a young woman dressed in a jacket and with a handbag slung over her shoulder pushed through into the room and turned to face her cases.

Their eyes met. Eloise froze. The air seemed to go still. Her mouth fell open in slow motion and a sound emerged that was little more than a long gasp, like a deflated, powerless scream dripping out onto the floor.

Then she was scrambling backwards for the door, losing her footing, kicking out in his direction, catching him cleanly in the face as he jumped up to reach her.

Slim grunted, seeing stars as the weight of her hips came behind the blow, but he moved on autopilot, aware he would get no other chance. He rode the blow, pushing through it, taking a second kick to the eye but catching her other ankle as she tried to get away. She was wearing jeans, giving him plenty of grip, so he wound her in, flipping her over as he did so to negate the power of her hands as she tried to fight him off.

His old army strength had all but gone, but he

remembered enough of studied wrestling tactics to pin her, holding her face down so she couldn't get out a scream loud enough to bring help.

He was half across her, using his body weight to hold her down. She was crying, a sound which sent tremors shuddering through his heart.

He understood now. The picture he had seen so briefly had explained so much. Explained why the girl was working at Greenway. Explained why she was never home.

'I won't hurt you,' he said. 'I'm so sorry, but I needed to talk. Please don't be afraid. I might look like shit warmed up on a grill but I'm no danger to you.'

Two girls, similar enough to be easily mistaken by a casual observer, arms around the other's shoulders, smiling into the camera.

'Who are you?' Lauren Trebuchet asked, her voice shaking with fear.

49

'You could have left a note,' Lauren said. 'I can read, you know. Was it really necessary to break in and then assault me in my own flat?'

Slim sighed. 'I'm sorry. But I wasn't looking for you, remember? I was looking for your sister. A girl who threatened to kill me and possibly even tried.'

It was Lauren's turn to sigh. 'She has a habit of doing things like that,' she said. 'That's why I followed her down here, because I was worried about Carson ... about her father.'

Lauren had found coffee from somewhere, heated over a little camping stove because she hadn't planned to stay long and was yet to bother getting the electricity switched on. Slim clutched a mug in two aching hands, having refused an offer of a wet towel to press against the bruise slowly closing up the eye the pub brawlers had missed.

Lauren, still glowering with anger, but at least no longer trying to kick his head off, sat across the room, legs pulled up in front of her, a cup of coffee held over her lap. Now that he saw her up close, Slim could tell them apart. Their features were similar, but Lauren was a little fuller in the face, her skin tone a little more Mediterranean than Eloise's British paleness. Her eyes, too, had none of the maniacal glare of her sister.

'We've known for a long time,' Lauren said. 'Our mother met him at a party in the late nineties.' She cracked one palm against her leg. 'Boom. Thirty minutes with a drunken radio celebrity and hallelujah, here's a daughter.'

'He had no part in her life?'

'None whatsoever. My mother never said a word until after the man we'd both always considered our father passed away from cancer when I was seventeen and Eloise fifteen. We weren't well off and I think Mum liked the idea of squeezing a little money out of Eloise's rich, famous real dad.'

'Did she get in contact with him?'

Lauren shrugged. 'She tried, but we never heard anything. No doubt all her attempts got blocked by the firewall of his management. For the record, I tried to talk her out of it. It was only going to make Eloise worse.'

'Worse?'

Lauren sighed. 'There were signs she was going off the rails a couple of years before Dad died. She was always into whatever caused trouble: drink, drugs, hanging with the wrong people. She started having destructive rages, followed by periods of seclusion where she refused to leave her room. She was eventually diagnosed as schizophrenic. Medication worked, but only when she took it. Dad's death levelled things up, though.

He had been the one calming influence in her life, the only person who had ever got through to her.' Lauren rolled her eyes. 'Eloise was institutionalised for the first time about a month after Dad's death. And that was before she even knew the truth.'

'You mean, into a psychiatric hospital?'

'Yeah. One in Exeter. My sister being my sister, she absolutely refused to cooperate. They had to sedate her a lot of the time. Mum was dealing with Dad's death, so I did most of the visiting to spare Mum the trauma. That led to Eloise's rejection of her. Dad was perfect, Dad was the best, while Mum was worthless.' Lauren flapped her hand. 'One day, Mum couldn't take it anymore. She blurted out that Eloise wasn't really Dad's daughter. My dad never knew. Mum had a certain type, and Dad and Carson didn't look a lot different. Dad died thinking Eloise was his.' Lauren sighed, her head slumping back against the wall with a soft bump. 'In the space of a year, we went from a normalish boring family to a complete cock-up.'

'It must have been hard on you.'

'I don't think I've ever had time to think about it properly. Six years now, Dad's been dead. Eloise has been in and out of hospitals and prisons. She doesn't talk to Mum and I only pass on vague details. I've given up on any kind of life for myself in order to look out for both of them. Eloise, though ... she's a force of nature. When she wants something ... it's hard to stop her.'

'I've been trying to track her down,' Slim said. 'It hasn't been easy.'

He had told Lauren who he was, and to his surprise had found the girl remembered his name from the papers a year back related to an old missing-persons case he had solved. It meant her trust had come easier than he might have hoped, even though she still eyed him with a wary sense of suspicion.

'I met a man she threatened to kill, and she told me herself about a man she left to die. She told me she went to prison.'

Lauren gave a frantic shake of her head. 'He didn't die. She got two years suspended for aggravated attempted manslaughter, but because he was deemed to have assaulted her she was effectively set free. The man was a nurse at the institution she was in at the time.' Her face hardened. 'He deserved it, if you ask me. He was convicted of six counts of assault on sedated female patients. He got fifteen years.'

Slim nodded. 'That's a level of justice at least.'

'Eloise always preferred her version. She's a chronic liar and a clever manipulator. I know she's my sister, but she's dangerous and I don't trust her. That's why I need to find her. Max Carson is dead. Her focus will be elsewhere now, perhaps trying to cover her tracks, deflect suspicion, maybe even trying to frame someone else.'

Slim had been holding off asking the question he had been aching to ask, but he could no longer resist.

'Do you think she killed him?'

Lauren lifted her head away from the wall. 'She was stalking him. Following him to work, hanging around outside his house. I warned her to leave him alone, but I couldn't bring myself to call the police on my own sister, even after everything she'd done. When she told me she'd signed up for a rehabilitation course in Dartmouth, I got suspicious. It wasn't like Eloise to have a sudden change of heart. I did some digging and found out Carson was also on the course.' She reached into her pocket and pulled out a phone. 'She wouldn't answer my calls, so I left her a message. This is the reply I received.'

Lauren held out the phone. Slim reached forward to take it, then turned it around to look. The words on the screen chilled him to the bone.

Next to a grinning devil emoji, the single sentence had been intentionally colored red.

I'll be saying goodbye to my father soon.

50

'Won't she have fled the area?' Slim asked. 'You said she left her bag behind.'

He had wondered how the strand of hair he had taken from the bag by the door had come up with a match to Carson when he shared no DNA with Lauren, but as Lauren explained, the bag had belonged to Eloise. Her sister had left it behind at the Castle View Hotel. When Lauren had contacted the tour company while looking for her sister, they had asked her to come and pick it up.

Lauren shook her head. 'She doesn't care much for material stuff. She'll buy or steal what she needs and then abandon it when she moves on. And she'll still be nearby, trust me. She loves to see the fallout of the trouble she causes. She's sadistic like that. No, she'll be somewhere nearby, hiding out, watching, waiting to see what happens.'

'How's she supporting herself?' he asked.

'That's what I'm trying to find out. She's gone to

ground. I've had no contact from her in weeks, nor has there been any sign of her. Nothing online, her phone's switched off. After her last bout of hospitalisation she was no longer allowed a solo bank account. We share one, but there's been no activity, no cash withdrawals except my own. I thought she might have been prostituting herself, because it wouldn't be the first time. I've spent so much time up in Exeter or over in Plymouth, trawling the seedy parts of town....' She shook her head. 'She's vanished.'

'Are you sure about Carson? I mean, she told me she had an alibi for that night. She said she was sleeping with the tour rep.'

'Another fanciful story, no doubt.'

'And I remember her reaction to the news. No shock or surprise. She asked me why I thought Carson had killed himself and then told me he had propositioned her, offered her money for sex.'

Lauren rubbed her eyes. 'Before the psychosis took hold, my sister was a good person,' Lauren said. 'After that ... she became destructive. Killing him might have been the end result, but she wouldn't have wanted it to be quick. She would have wanted him to suffer, wanted to see the hurt and fear in his eyes.'

'Could she have seduced him and then taken him up to Greenway where his body was found? You see, of everything I've figured out, one thing is still a massive stumbling block to any theory. How did they get out there? It's a couple of miles upriver, and no ferries run at that time of night.'

Lauren shook her head. 'You're the detective, not me. I'm just trying to find my sister.'

Slim considered mentioning his mysterious benefactor, but decided against it. It had crossed his mind that Lauren herself might be responsible, as she had regular access to Greenway, but the DNA had ruled her out.

'I have to go to bed,' Lauren said at last, and Slim realised they had talked long after midnight. 'I have work tomorrow.'

Slim didn't waste time telling her he was essentially homeless. In her shoes he would have wanted him out as soon as possible. He nodded, standing up.

'Can I contact you?' he said. 'If there are any developments?'

Lauren nodded. 'Sure.' She gave him her number, expressing surprise at his lack of a phone. At the door, she wished him good luck.

Slim once again found himself shut out into the night. Weary beyond words, he took a meandering, winding route through Paignton's backstreets before finally reaching the tiny bus station. The waiting room was locked, the little café still a couple of hours from opening. Slim stared at a couple of homeless by the wall beneath the shelter of the bus ports, shifting uncomfortably in dirty sleeping bags. He had no desire to hunker down with them so he retreated up the road, trying to ward off the cold with continual movement.

There was no shelter anywhere, no late night cafés or petrol stations. He was staring at a small luminous glow at the end of a side street when the ground around him began to patter with rain.

The light came from a phone box. Slim squeezed inside, enjoying the brief respite from the gusting wind and the dampening rain which had left his face slick. He wiped himself down with a sleeve then stared out at the night as the rain grew heavier. It was ridiculous to think of standing here all night, but at least it was shelter. He crouched down into the floor space, trying to draw up his knees to rest his legs and conserve a little heat. He had just leaned his head against the glass when a car turned into the street.

The flickering lights on its roof made Slim stand up quickly. He picked up the receiver and pretended to speak as the car slowed. He turned his head, pretending not to see it, hoping it would just pass him by. His heart thundered, his hand shaking so badly he could barely keep the receiver pressed to his ear.

At the very moment his nerves gave out and he dropped the receiver with a noisy rattle, the police car picked up speed, reaching the end of the road and turning left. Slim considered fleeing before they made another pass, but there was no cover nearby, nowhere to hide. Instead, he leaned down to retrieve the receiver.

As he did so, something fell out of his jacket.

The beer mat. Slim picked it up and turned it over, staring at the phone number written on the underside.

He didn't know the time, but it was an inappropriate time to call anyone. Except, he had picked the number up in a bar, and if ever there was a number to be called in the middle of the night, it was one written on the back of a bar mat in red ink.

As flashing lights appeared at the far end of the street, indicating the police car was back for another run, Slim slipped a pound into the slot and dialled the number.

It rang only twice before a woman's voice came on the other end.

'Hello? Do you know why you're calling me?'

The ease with which the woman spoke made Slim's fingers tremble. He knew immediately what kind of woman he had called. One who might be holed up sleeping during the day, but came alive at night.

'Yes,' he said. 'I do.'

'So tell me, sir, how and when would you like to have your private audience with Beatrice Winter?'

51

I need money, Slim wrote. *And I need to know who you are. I can't play this game anymore.*

He tucked the note into the basket and left it inside the door.

He made a point of avoiding Greenway, taking a circuitous route down to the pier for Dartmouth and catching a ferry headed downriver.

He was almost out of money, but he no longer cared. He spent what little he had left on a decent ready-meal out of a small supermarket which he hoped wouldn't taste too bad cold, then headed for an Internet café located in a basement room beneath a bookshop.

Lauren had given him a list of Eloise's medications, and the addresses of several institutions where she had spent time. He spent a couple of hours reading up on what he could find, but a lot of the medical information was technical jargon, while each institution's website obviously glossed over their darker innards. He needed to contact them directly, so noted down their emails and reluctantly opened his own, aware he would be leaving a trail for police to follow. Once opened, however, he was unable to deny his natural curiosity at the list of unopened messages. Many were circulars, but only yesterday he had received one from Kim with URGENT PLEASE OPEN!! as the subject line. Unable to resist, he dutifully opened the email.

Slim, where in heaven's name are you? If you're still able to read this, you have to contact me. I don't like to say this, but I think your life is in danger.

Usually so level-headed, the urgency in Kim's words left him concerned. He didn't reply, but instead went outside, walked down to the waterfront and found a phone box on the edge of the Royal Avenue Gardens.

It felt strange to dial his office number after so long. He didn't expect Kim to actually answer. With all the ongoing drama he would have forgiven her for simply walking away, so when she answered with a crisp, 'John Hardy Private Investigation Services, how may I help you today?' he was too stunned to immediately reply.

'Excuse me? Is there anybody there? How may I help?'

The suave, noir comeback would have been to give a breathy one-liner, but Slim was instead racked by a sudden burst of coughing. He held the receiver against his chest until it had subsided. When he returned it to his ear, the first thing he heard was, 'I think you need to see a doctor.'

'Kim, it's me.'

'I know it is. Where in heaven's name have you been? People have been worried—well, I've been worried; your non-existent social circle keeps you in the clear otherwise. What do you think you're playing at? I've had all manner of people wanting to speak to you, and—'

'The police?'

'Yes, they called a few times, but not of late. I've had plenty of others, though. Clients you've left in the lurch, a couple from friends of yours, wanting to know why you've not been answering your phone—'

'Ben Holland? Did he call?'

'Yes, a few days ago. He said someone would be in touch.'

Slim's heart skipped a beat. Could his mysterious benefactor be a police officer? He was still staring off into space, mulling over the possibility, when Kim said, 'It was the letter I needed to speak to you about.'

'What letter?'

'It arrived yesterday. It's signed by someone called Eloise.'

His heart skipped another beat. He wasn't sure how many more shocks he could take before the abused old thing gave up on him.

'The postmark?'

'Dartmouth. A week ago, so it must have got stuck somewhere.'

'What does it say?'

'"*Dear Slim, I just wanted to let you know that you're being watched. You might think that you're above the law, but you're not. I know what you did. And I know where you are now. If you turn around quick enough, you'll see me watching. And you'll see in my eyes that I know what you did. And you'll also see there what I'm going to do to you soon, when I'm ready. Yours, kindly, Eloise.*"'

The way Kim managed to replicate the menacing

tone of Eloise's words made him shiver, reminding him that the girl was out there somewhere. And now he knew for certain that she was hunting him even as he was hunting her.

'I think you should stop whatever it is you're doing and come back,' Kim said. 'Talk to the police. Deal with whatever concerns they have and let them look into this. I'm worried for you, Mr. Hardy. This girl sounds serious. She hasn't even bothered to hide her identity. Do you know her?'

Slim nodded into the phone. 'I've met her,' he said, deciding to keep the details brief. 'And I'm aware how dangerous she is.'

'Then come back.'

'I can't. What I'm doing right now, it's ... important.'

'Are you sure about that?'

The phone gave a tired bleep, the display counting down the last seconds before his money ran out.

'Kim, I—'

Too late. The only answer was an empty dial tone.

52

THE STREET WAS LITTLE MORE THAN AN ALLEYWAY LEADING sharply uphill from the main road, with several parked cars sitting unevenly on the cobblestones, pressed tightly in against the walls. Slim paused by an old Ford, its wheel arches flecked with rust, and peered again at the address he had written on the beer mat above the telephone number.

This was the place. He squeezed past the car to the house, briefly catching the hem of his jacket on the corner of a boot door that didn't shut properly and having to pull it free. The door bobbed up, revealing a pile of old fishing nets on the lowered back seat. With an embarrassed grimace, he pushed it back down, clicking it half-shut as it had been before.

The bell rang with a lethargic drone. Like the car boot he presumed belonged to the same person, the front door didn't shut properly. Slim slid his fingers into the gap until the lock came loose, then pushed the door open to reveal several bubbling fish tanks in a gloomy hallway which contained all manner of sea life. He stepped back outside, checking the number on the door to make sure he hadn't made a mistake.

'Um ... Beatrice?' he called into the gloom.

'Come to the top of the stairs,' said a woman's voice. 'I'm waiting for you. The second door on the left.'

Slim did as he was instructed, passing more fish tanks standing on the stairs. Halfway up he paused to look at a small stingray circling an undersized tank perched precariously on a stack of bricks painted luminous green.

On the landing, sand crunched beneath his feet, and old fishing nets decorated the walls. The correct door was identified by a string of shells hung from a hook and a welcome sign decorated with pieces of coral. A mermaid painted in faded watercolours had a hand lifted in a wave. Slim paused to touch the string of shells, feeling their graininess, noticing the dust in their cracks. Then he opened the door.

He found himself in a mock underwater scene, like a stage setup for a theatre performance. In the middle, a regular double bed was surrounded by piled sea buoys and exotic shells draped with fishing nets. It smelled like a quayside tourist shop. Pebbles and sand covered the uneven floor. Cool aquamarine lamps hidden by overflowing treasure chests backlit everything.

'Payment is required upfront,' a voice said from behind a curtain.

Slim jumped back as the curtain parted enough to reveal a veiled face, the body still hidden. The woman chuckled.

'All first-timers react like that. Now, tell me what you want from these.' She held up a piece of laminate which, from the way it was creased, its edges frayed, had clearly been perused a countless number of times. The pictures at the top, of a series of themed outfits, had faded, while the list of sordid activities written in pen underneath was barely legible from where the plastic laminate had come unstuck from the paper beneath.

'I only want to talk,' Slim said.

The woman chuckled again. 'That's what they all say,' she said. 'Take off your jacket and wait over there. I'll give you a basic package. Half price, since it's your first time, and a shy man always turns me on.'

Slim handed over a clutch of banknotes. It was most of what he had found in the basket this morning, even though his benefactor had declined to answer any of his questions.

The woman pocketed the money, then went through a door behind the curtain. Slim took off his clothes as the woman had asked, leaving on only a t-shirt and his jeans. He sat down on the edge of the bed and waited.

From somewhere behind him, a tape recorder clicked and the room filled with the sound of waves crashing onto a shore, punctuated by the odd cry of a gull. The lights dimmed. Slim watched the door uncomfortably, feeling less turned on and more part of a bizarre circus. He was just wondering whether to cut his losses and bail, when the door opened and the woman reappeared.

Her face was again veiled, but the rest of her was now visible. She wore a flowing wig of golden braids that draped over otherwise bare breasts. She was naked to the waist, but from there wore a sky blue skirt of glittery material that covered her feet. She shuffled forward, and only as she came into the circle of light did Slim understand why she wasn't walking properly: the skirt was sewn together at the bottom, before fanning out again in a representation of a fish's silvery tale.

'Beatrice Winter,' Slim said. 'Old Bea.'

'Less of the old, please,' the woman said, lowering herself down beside him. 'Well, look at you. You like to work out, don't you?'

Slim, who hadn't been near a gym in years, scoffed at what was an obvious line. 'I'm a functioning alcoholic,' he said.

'And a real charmer,' the woman added with a smirk. 'Why don't you just let me relax you?' She tried to ease Slim down on to his back, but he resisted.

'A mermaid,' he said. 'Is that what they claimed she was?'

The woman's hands continued to work, but Slim noticed how her fingers had tensed as she massaged his shoulders.

'To whom are you referring, darling?'

'Beatrice. Old Bea. There was something wrong with her, wasn't there?'

'Look—'

'I'll pay extra if you tell me what you know.'

The woman's hands paused before they began to work again. She let out a sigh, then said, her voice reverting to character, 'My great-great-grandmother, the original Beatrice, was a wonder of the sea. Some say a siren, others a mermaid. Perplexing sailors all along the Dart River valley. Some say she climbed onto boats to pleasure weary travellers, others that she waited by the docks for the boats to come in.'

'She wasn't really a mermaid, was she?'

The woman sighed. 'You're not making this easy, are you?' Reverting again to character, she added, 'She could swim with a speed and grace few could believe.'

'But she could walk on land like a woman, and have sex with sailors like a woman. Why did they call her a sea witch?'

The woman's hands stopped moving and she let out a sigh. 'I don't think this is working, do you?'

'I'm sorry,' Slim said. 'I just wanted to know about Old Bea. I thought you might know something. This is just a circus act, isn't it?'

Suddenly finding her modesty, the woman removed her wig and the veil attached to it, and held it over her exposed chest. Slim looked into the eyes of a woman in her early fifties, ruffled light brown hair starting to grey, face a little sour, skin a little worn.

'Would you like a drink?' she asked.

Slim gave a grim smile. 'Finally something I understand,' he said.

53

He sat with his legs dangling out over the edge of the pier. His head thudded from the cheap navy rum the woman named Kirsten had produced, which she told him was sometimes used to soften nervy customers, and he was pleased he had given her the last of his money as a bonus, to prevent him from buying more. After the first glass, his tongue had loosened and he had laid his soul bare, explaining that he was a private investigator trying to unravel the mysterious deaths of two people in Dartmouth a couple of months ago, an investigation that was going nowhere.

And another piece of the puzzle had fallen into place.

By the time half the bottle was gone, Kirsten's tongue had also loosened enough to release its own bombshell.

'He came here that night,' she slurred. 'He got my number from someone in a bar and showed up at my door. He told me two women he was with had pulled a runner on him. I did what I do and then we got talking. He was interested in much of the same stuff you were.'

'About Old Bea?'

She gave a nervous laugh. 'But less of the historical side. I got the impression he had a bit of a ... deviant streak. We talked a bit, and we got on to her supposed daughter, Eliza. I told him what little I knew, and somewhere along the line he started on about seeing where she died.'

'Eliza?'

Kirsten nodded. 'He offered me far more money than I'd usually get for a night's work. Not the kind of sum I can afford to turn down. I saw a couple of nights off and perhaps even a new set of tyres for that banger out the front there, so I took him up there.'

'To Greenway? By boat?'

Kirsten had laughed at this. 'Do I look like a sailor? Of course not. I drove, in that piece of junk I call a car. It's been out of MOT for the last couple of months, but the money he offered was worth risking the police. The biggest surprise was that we made it.'

By road. The obvious way, the one Slim had overlooked.

'It was getting light by the time we arrived. We parked where the ferry docks and walked through the woods. He was fascinated by the place. He wanted to have sex on the old bridge there, while the sun came up. I agreed, but then he squatted down and held up a ball of twine. I don't know where it came from, whether he had it all along or he'd found it somewhere, but he tied it around his ankles then said he wanted me to do the same. Some weird kink thing, so we could screw like mermaids, or whatever. At my place I would have likely gone for it—encouraged it, even—but out there in the middle of nowhere, I got spooked, so I refused. He got angry, so I ran. He was drunk, his ankles were already tied, and so he had no chance of catching me. I left him there, and tried to forget about it until I saw the news reports of his death.'

'And you didn't go to the police?'

Kirsten rolled her eyes. 'I'm a middle-aged prostitute who dresses as a mermaid. They'd have booked me or laughed at me. They never came knocking, so I figured I was clear. I had nothing to do with his death. It's just that, in my ... business ... you meet a lot of people on the verge of something. Desperate people. People wanting something but not quite sure what it is.'

'People like me?'

Kirsten laughed. 'If there was a mould, you'd be a perfect fit. That's why I told you. Perhaps that's what you were looking for.'

Slim smiled at the memory. Kirsten had known him as he walked through the door. And while it was true that the information was a massive boost, it left him no closer to finding out what had happened to Carson.

Dead with string tied around his ankles, allegedly tied himself. The obvious answer was that Kirsten had left things unsaid, that she had perhaps allowed the game to go on longer before making her break for freedom. Slim, though, knew how well a bit of drink worked to bring out the truth, and had seen no lies in her face. She had told him straight, as best as she remembered it. Carson had met his demise after she had left. But an unfortunate accident, suicide, or murder, he was no closer to finding out.

Kirsten driving Carson out to Greenaway solved the problem of how he had got there. What it didn't do, however, was link Eloise with a possible murder. Was it likely the girl had somehow followed them? Or had she perhaps guessed what Carson would do and lain in wait? Or was she now absolved of any association?

He remembered her first message to him: *I'll kill you for what you did.* Did she blame Slim for a murder she had wanted but missed the opportunity to commit for herself?

He squeezed his temples, his head aching more than ever.

54

Suicides. Witches. Mermaids. Slim stared at the words he had scribbled on a piece of paper before ripping it off the notepad and screwing it up. He glanced up at the café's service counter but no one was paying him any attention. Picking up his pen, he began to jot notes and draw connecting lines all over again.

An hour of fruitless consideration later, he stepped out into a rainy morning. He let out a long, rasping series of coughs he had suppressed in the café's quiet confines, stumbled down to Kingswear's ferry port, and took a boat across the river to Dartmouth.

By the time he got off the ferry, the rain had got heavier. Not in the mood for huddling in shop doorways, and finding each café he passed crowded with sheltering tourists, he caught a local bus headed for Dartmouth's new fishing heritage museum, which he was yet to visit.

Located at the southern edge of the estuary-hugging town on the road heading to the castle, Slim found its modern, Perspex corridors drab and unbefitting of a museum, perhaps explaining the dearth of customers as he wandered from one lifeless display to another. Light on the surface, each display told a history book rendition of the town's industrial and fishing past, slowly leading to its transformation into an exclusive haunt of the rich and their marinas. There was little Slim hadn't heard or read before, so when he spotted an arrow pointing to a cafeteria, he headed that way, pleased to see it sold soft drinks only, quieting the beast he had awoken the night before and which now sat on his shoulder, whispering temptations which would end this nightmare for good. After a relapse it was sometimes there, sometimes not, but he sensed this time he had gone too far, and that it wouldn't leave without a fight.

There was only one other customer, a young man reading a newspaper. Slim was within a couple of steps of the counter when he caught a glimpse of the man's face in a mirror behind the serving bar.

Alex Wade from the tour company.

Slim backed away, a survival instinct kicking in. Alex would surely recognise him, and if there was anyone outside the police who knew what he was being accused of, it was the tour company rep.

Ignoring the bemused frown on the server's face, Slim backed up, pushing through the closest door he could reach to put himself out of sight.

He had expected a toilet or emergency exit, but instead found himself in a stock room with dimmed lights. As he took in his surroundings, he realised the room must supply both the cafeteria and an adjacent gift shop, with industrial-sized cans of tomato ketchup standing alongside boxes of trinkets and embossed tea towels.

He moved through the room towards the other door, marvelling at the kind of things customers rarely saw splurging out of the open tops of boxes. There were other things not boxed too: delicate handmade ornaments and a cluster of paintings wrapped in cellophane which appeared ready for display.

He paused to look at one, feeling an uneasy sense of familiarity. It showed a downriver view of the Dart Estuary, with Kingswear visible to the left, slightly clearer than Dartmouth to the right, appearing hazier as though caught in morning mist. The painter: Alan McDonald.

Slim was still staring at the painting when the door opened behind him. 'You're not allowed back here,' someone said.

Without turning around, Slim lifted a hand. 'I'm sorry,' he said. 'I took the wrong door by mistake.'

Before the person behind him could say anything else, he moved quickly away from the paintings, out through a door that emerged into a brightly lit gift shop. Customers filled the narrow aisles, practically climbing over each other to view the lines of history books and racks of postcards. From the haunted look in the eyes that met his, Slim recognised them as Alex's current tour party, and not wishing to spend longer among them than necessary, he eased his way through the throng to a door leading outside.

The road sloped away, seemingly about to drop into the estuary below before abruptly cutting back on itself and disappearing out of sight. A pub hugged the corner, a signboard outside naming it as THE LOOKOUT: DARTMOUTH'S MOST SCENIC BEER GARDEN.

The thought of an afternoon of oblivion made Slim's eyes water. His resolve all but broken by days sleeping rough and a sickness that wouldn't let go, he would have headed straight for the bar with the handful of change he had left, had it not been for the police car parked up at the roadside beside the museum's small car park, and WPC Marion Oaks leaning against the front door, casually reading a museum pamphlet. As he stepped forward, she looked up. No surprise registered in her eyes as she stepped away from the door and said, 'I wondered how long it would take you to get through that pokey little place. Get in.'

55

'I suppose I would have been rumbled in the end,' Marion said, turning the police car into a lane that cut up through trees towards the hilltop. 'Your utter incompetence forced my hand. I couldn't risk someone else picking you up.'

'You're the one who's been leaving things for me?'

Marion shrugged. 'If you think you're equipped to survive living rough in that place, you're doing a poor job of showing it.'

'I set traps—'

'I know. I watched you doing it.'

'Watched me?'

'There are cameras. You were watching your traps, Slim. You weren't watching for those already set.'

'Cameras?'

'That house is private property. It has security cameras. They're just hidden well to stop them getting stolen, and frankly, some have got a little damaged over the years. It's been a while since my father checked or adjusted them.'

'Your father? But Greenway ... the National Trust—'

'Owns the land as far as the old railway cutting. The rest was auctioned off back in the 1950s, including the land on which that old house stands.'

'Your father—'

Marion nodded. 'Actually, my grandfather bought it. I think at one time he thought he could turn the riverside land into a small marina, but he never found the time or money, and it's pretty much stayed as it was the day he bought it. I did wonder about renovating the property one day when my father passes, but the cost would be prohibitive. The land is prone to subsidence due to its proximity to the river. It would take serious construction to make it safe.' Marion sighed. 'But I digress.'

'If there are cameras—' Slim began, then realised he was getting ahead of himself. 'Why help me? Why not just arrest me for trespassing?' He remembered an angry old woman once claiming a fine of up to five grand could be issued for trespass; surely by now he'd be close to the top end.

'Because you wanted to know the answer. The deaths of both Irene Long and Max Carson have been classified as suicides. Their cases have been officially closed.' Marion had turned off the lane onto what was little more than a dirt road. Branches brushed at the car's sides as they continued steadily uphill.

'But you don't believe it.'

'There are fingers in too many pies,' Marion continued. 'People don't want an investigation.'

'The council?'

Marion's laugh took Slim by surprise. When she glanced at him, she even had a tear in her eye. 'Come on, TV detective. You really think?'

'The yachting clubs. The people with real money.'

'Bingo.'

'You're taking backhanders?'

Marion laughed again. 'Nothing so sinister. Veiled threats to remove funding from community projects. To withdraw long-term leases on community-used land. To build car parks over parks and put people out of jobs. To screw up the lives of those of us poor enough to have to live here all year round.'

'But you don't care. You think Long and Carson were murdered. You want to keep the investigation open.'

'There is evidence to suggest neither death was a suicide. And it goes against my integrity as a police officer to let this case go.'

'You have evidence that your superiors suppressed to keep the yachting clubs happy?'

Marion rolled her eyes as she turned the car through an open farm entrance and bounced to a stop behind a thick, overgrown hedgerow.

'You watch too much TV. Nothing was suppressed. It was just considered of too little value to investigate further. Manpower, resources. The usual excuses.'

'So you let me keep my investigation open?'

Marion turned to face him. 'At first I thought you were a rough sleeper. I actually did go out there to arrest you, take you somewhere a little less harsh. Possibly, given what else I've heard about you, somewhere with bars over the windows. Then I got a phone call from an old friend.'

'Ben.'

Marion nodded. 'Ben Holland was my class director at training college. He is a man I have a deep respect for, so when he told me an acquaintance of his was looking into the Carson case, I put two and two together. You were together in the military?'

'Same platoon in the first Gulf War. He did a lot better afterwards than I did.'

'Come on, Slim. You didn't do too bad. Even I'd heard of you. You've closed some cases that couldn't be closed.'

'I've got lucky.'

'The harder you work, the luckier you seem to get. My experience at any rate.'

Slim shrugged. 'Well, I can't have worked hard enough on this case.'

'Hopefully I can help with that.' She reached into a briefcase at her feet and withdrew a paper folder. 'These are the case notes I could get copies of. Autopsy reports, that kind of thing. We didn't have enough to nail anything down, but if there are things you've discovered that we haven't....'

He took the offered folder and laid it across his lap. 'Thanks.'

She sighed, staring out of the windscreen at the view down over the Dart valley. 'I need to cut ties with you, Slim,' she said. 'I'm putting my career on the line doing this, and I can't afford to get caught. I'm sorry. I have two young children....'

Slim nodded. 'I understand. Do you want me to leave the house?'

Marion shook her head. 'I can give you another week.

There's a warrant out for your arrest. Keep your head down.'

'The misdemeanours—'

Marion put up a hand. 'Whatever you find, take it to a higher authority. Take it direct to Cornwall and Devon Constabulary in Plymouth. It might get you an easier run.'

Slim wasn't sure he believed that, but it sounded that he was in the clear for suspicion of murder at least. He would deal with the rest when it came to it.

'Can I leave you here?' Marion said, nodding at the door. 'I fear being seen with you, and I've disabled radio contact long enough that my sarge might ask questions.'

'Sure.' Slim started to open the door, then paused. 'One thing, please. I saw you, that first night.'

'You saw me?'

'I was drunk, delirious. I saw a figure dive into the water. It was you, wasn't it?'

'Slim....'

'Tell me, damn you. I can't solve anything if I'm forever drowning in secrets. I thought you must have had a boat, but you were naked, I was sure of it. It made no sense at the time, and it makes little now, but ... you swam across that river, didn't you? Somehow you swam across that river.'

Marion stared at him for several seconds. Slim expected her to brush him off, or worse, renege on her decision to help him and arrest him instead.

'None of us are perfect,' she said at last. 'At least by society's standards. But then, sometimes what we believe is a curse might actually be a gift. Your drinking, for example.'

Slim held her stare, understanding. 'I despise it,' he said, 'and I despise myself every time I stumble, every time I go back to it. It'll kill me one day, I'm sure, but sometimes ... there are cases I wouldn't have solved without the insight it gives me, that alternative train of thought. I dream of leaving it behind, but sometimes I wonder ... if I would be leaving behind a part of what I am. What made me.'

Marion shifted in the seat and Slim frowned, wondering if something in his words had made her flinch. Then, as she leaned down, reaching into the foot well, he realised what she had done.

Kicked off her shoe.

'I have my own curse,' she said, pulling off a sock to reveal a pale white foot. 'One which, in certain circumstances, could be considered a gift. From a great-great-grandmother, down to me.'

Slim stared. Marion flexed her toes, and there, extending between each, Slim saw perfect semi-circles of skin.

56

'Webbed feet?'

Slim nodded. 'I need to know if that's some kind of hereditary condition, and anything you can find on it. Recorded medical case studies, names of people afflicted, literally anything.'

'Slim ... are you sure you're all right down there? I mean, this is pretty out-there stuff.'

'Don, I know it. I'm at a point where I can't believe anything I hear or read, but if I sift through enough dirt, I might find gold.'

'You know how many prospectors probably said that, and how many actually found it?'

Slim gave the phone a tired smile. 'I don't, but I expect you could tell me.'

'Almost all of them. You could quit on this one, you know. Sometimes a case can't be closed.'

'I know that too. I'm giving it another week, then I'm done.'

'Well, call me back tomorrow. I'll pull an all-nighter if I have to, but you'll owe me for this.'

'I'll add it to the account.'

'Speak soon, Slim.'

Don hung up. Slim sighed as he stared at the payphone handset, wondering if Don was right. Perhaps he should save himself a fruitless week and walk into the nearest police station, face whatever music was due, and perhaps get a decent wash.

He took a ferry back across the river to Kingswear, holing himself up in his favourite café to look over the notes Marion had given him.

It was as she had said, mostly trivial stuff, crime scene photographs, autopsy reports for both Max Carson and Irene Long, the results of blood samples, transcripts of interviews with a number of people who might have seen either in their last few days. Slim was amused to find his own interview in there, but of the others there was little revelation: most were interviews with other tour customers, as well as some hotel staff and the two tour reps. Slim browsed them one by one, finding nothing noteworthy; Carson had raised a few hackles but had done nothing worse than act with the obnoxiousness his reputation suggested.

And concerning Irene, there was only Slim's interview to work with. Marion had included a few scribbled notes mentioning possible sightings, but it was clear that of the two, Irene's death had been far more quickly written off as suicide. Slim stared at the autopsy report, wondering what he might be missing. Blood tests revealed Irene had been on several types of medication, as she had told him herself. He could no longer recall the names of any, nor even if she had told him. In any case, they were listed only as chemical components, rather than brands or common store-used names.

He scratched a mark beside them with a pencil. It might be worth checking, just in case.

So Carson had gone out there to the old bridge because he wanted to screw a mermaid. It was unique, for certain, albeit—having briefly met the man—something Slim could believe. For a philandering, drug-addicted radio host with a history of affairs and misdemeanours, it was almost trivial.

But somehow he had ended up dead.

Eloise, the daughter Carson didn't know existed, had a personal vendetta on his head. She had planned to kill him, but maybe she thought someone else had got there first.

I'll kill you for what you did.

Slim frowned.

He had been interviewed before anyone else, called away while in the middle of a conversation with the girl.

Was it possible Eloise hadn't killed Max Carson after all, but believed that Slim had? Had she had tried to kill him for supposedly denying her the chance of revenge?

He rubbed his temples, wishing there was some way to make sense of it all. Marion's revelation gave some credence to the myths of Eliza Turkin and Beatrice Winter. Two women with an unnaturally strong ability to swim, giving rise to the tales of them as both mermaids and sea witches. But was it something else, something perhaps genetic, which had caused the deformation? Something that, upon its appearance in a newborn, could fuel stories of a curse, one which had seen Beatrice

Winter outcast and her property burned, and had tarred Eliza Turkin by association before she was old enough to even understand why?

Slim wanted to bang his head on the tabletop. Too much history when all he was trying to do was figure out a simple murder case.

Or was it simple?

Perhaps for clarification, at the top of the police file was a typed list of names of people considered persons of interest. They had been separated into subgroups—the tour party, associates, locals who might have come into contact with either Carson or Long. Slim reached into his pocket and pulled out his own list, torn and water-stained, written in pen that had smudged in places, one containing all the persons he had himself considered of interest. He had of course added historical characters such as Eliza Turkin and Beatrice Winter. There were some crossovers, such as Alex Wade and Jane Hounslow from the tour party, others that existed on his list but not on Marion's, such as the painter, Alan McDonald, and the same could be said of hers. As Slim scanned them, he tried to spot connections he had missed, people he hadn't considered that the police might have, connections between the names.

And there it was, staring him in the face.

Winter.

Beatrice Winter, the prostitute and—depending on your point of view—a suspected mermaid or even sea witch.

If Marion was a descendent of Winter, it made sense that she had married out of her family name, or perhaps dropped it altogether. But what if the claim that Beatrice had multiple children was true, and her later-generation descendants chose instead to retain a portion of their family history, out of respect or reverence?

The fisherman, who had run the tour excursion, a man Slim had briefly suspected of following him.

Winters.

Terrance Winters.

57

The tackle shop was closed, which wasn't unusual for a Sunday, Slim thought, as he made his way down a side alleyway, looking for lights or other signs of occupation in the adjoining cottage. The only side window was one of frosted glass, and the back was a white-washed stone wall surrounding a small, enclosed garden which bordered the rear of the house, too high to see over, and entered only through an old latched door fastened on the outside by a clunky padlock. Slim had his lock pick with him, but the rusty padlock would only respond to a pair of bolt cutters.

It looked like Terrance was out, perhaps enjoying some free time on the river. Slim glanced left and right, checking he was alone in the alley and that no one might be spying on him from any nearby buildings. Satisfied, he reached up, felt the top of the wall for anything unsavoury like embedded glass, then hauled himself up, every muscle in his body complaining as he slung himself in an ungainly manner over the top.

He landed heavily in a paved yard, then took a couple of minutes to rub his sore lower back while he looked around him.

The yard showed all the signs of a single man's life focused around a simple hobby. Along the back wall of the property were several open sheds filled with old maritime goods and trophies: sea buoys with faded colours, old lobster pots, interestingly shaped lumps of driftwood, pieces of fishing net, rusted lumps of metal which could have come from shipwrecks, and all manner of other bits and pieces a dedicated fisherman might have found in or near the sea.

To get to the back door, Slim had to step around a couple of small rowing boats in various stages of repair. There, his lock pick worked with its usual precision on a Yale lock, and he let himself into a gloomy dining room which smelled of cigarettes and coffee.

Certain the rear of Terrance's house was hidden from any neighbouring properties, Slim allowed himself the luxury of switching on a light, covering his fingertips with the cloth of his shirt in case his entry was later discovered. With the glow of an uncovered sixty-watt bulb pushing the shadows into the room's corners, he confirmed his suspicions: Terrance's life had the complete absence of a woman's touch. On a round table against a rear window covered by a dirty net curtain, a *Sun* newspaper lay open on page three, beside a coffee cup with a dried residue at the bottom, and an ashtray that either hadn't been emptied in several days, or marked Terrance as a heavy smoker. Slim frowned, remembering the inhaler he had seen that had marked Terrance as an asthmatic. Glancing around, he found it lying discarded in a bowl on the lower shelf of a dresser, beside an unopened pack of mints and half a pack of batteries. Slim used his sleeve to pick it up, gave it a press and smelled stale air but nothing else. A prop then, perhaps used to fake a condition.

Certain now it had been Terrance who had followed him in the forest back in the early days of his tour but unable to say why, Slim continued with even more caution. Hanging from a string on the wall was a tide-table book open on the current month, several tide times circled in black biro, indicating where Terrance had gone today. Taking each step carefully, Slim took in Terrance's life, eyes scanning the walls, getting a picture of the man. Clearly Terrance had an invested, almost religious interest in the River Dart, with framed historical photographs hanging from the walls, a tatty terrain map of the river valley tacked to a closed door, and several memorabilia pieces on a mantel which were labelled with loving care not evident elsewhere. One amorphous chunk of driftwood about the size of Slim's fist was labelled as part of the first steamship to dock at Dartmouth Harbour; while a rusty steel tube had apparently come from the wreck of a Second World War vessel that had run aground on the cliffs near Dartmouth Castle. Family photographs or personal mementoes were few and far between, but there was one dusty fly fishing prize from 1986, and a couple of black and white pictures of a young boy standing beside an older couple. Slim leaned closer to look, surmising that the woman was much older than the man, perhaps suggesting three generations. The man looked vaguely familiar, while the boy Slim guessed was Terrance.

The door with the map attached led off to the side, away from the shop entrance. Slim covered his hand with his sleeve again and opened it, stepping inside and closing it again before switching on a light.

He blinked. In sharp contrast to the clutter of Terrance's dining room, this room looked plucked right out of an art gallery, with a simple desk at one end and a couple of cupboards, surrounded on every available space by colourful paintings of the river valley.

The newest arrival lay on a small rectangular table in the room's centre, inside an open cardboard box. It showed a view of the Dart Valley looking downriver towards Dartmouth and Kingswear. Slim recognised it immediately as the same painting he had seen in the back room at the museum.

An Alan McDonald, a painting of an almost identical view to that which Slim saw each morning from the upper floor of Eliza Turkin's old house, but from lower down.

The waterline.

And the light, the shadows falling over the hills to the west, suggested it was an early morning view.

A handwritten note lay beside it.

Lad, just finished this one. Really proud of it. What do you think?

Slim felt his cheeks flush. How long did it take to finish a painting of this quality? A week? A month?

Could it put Alan McDonald at the scene of Max Carson's death?

Slim looked up. Now that he looked closer, he realised every single hung painting was an Alan McDonald original. A stack of several others stood against the wall, as though they reached Terrance faster than he could find places to hang them.

The man in the picture on the dining room mantel, he now recognised. Alan McDonald, far younger, with an ease to his features no longer present. The older woman had to be Corrine, his mother. And if the boy was Terrance—

His son?

Slim shook his head, thoughts and ideas swirling. He was still staring at the painting when the door clicked open behind him.

Time seemed to slow. Slim felt numb and immobile as Terrance Winters stepped into the room, pulling off a deerstalker hat as he did so. Terrance looked up, clocked Slim standing by the table, and his eyes widened.

'What the hell are you doing in here?' he said.

58

Terrance turned, but Slim's old military reflexes made him quicker. He got a grip on Terrance's jacket lapels and hauled him to the floor, wrapping his arms around the fisherman and pinning his arms beneath him. Slim felt Terrance's strength as the fisherman tried to kick him off, and knew in a straight fist fight he had no chance. What he did have was training—however long ago—and he used the old techniques to his advantage. Keeping Terrance pinned, he locked his hands together and held on, waiting for the stronger man to tire.

'Get the hell off me,' Terrance growled, his struggles growing weaker. 'What do you want from me? I'll call the police—'

'I'll be doing that myself,' Slim said, mouth close to Terrance's ear, trying to summon as much menace as he could. 'Accessory to murder? You could go down for five years, minimum. Ten if you're connected to others.'

'What are you talking about? What murder?'

'We talk like men, or I tie you like a pig and call you

in,' Slim said. 'I'm a private investigator, not connected to the police. I can make evidence against you disappear if I get the information I want.'

'What evidence? What are you talking about?'

'Or I could get you put away tomorrow.'

'How do I know you're not lying?'

'You don't,' Slim said. 'That's the chance you take. I won't be taking any, though. I have a friend in the police on speed dial, a pre-recorded voicemail ready to go at the push of a button. I can have them outside in five minutes. You wouldn't get to the end of the street.'

Threats made up on the spot, but he guessed correctly that Terrance's knowledge of technology extended no further than fishing tackle. Below him, the other man went limp.

'I need a cigarette,' Terrance said. 'That all right by you?'

'I can manage. All I want is answers to my questions. If you don't have all of them, it doesn't matter. As long as you have enough.'

～

'Why did you follow me that day?' Slim said. 'And why the ruse with the inhaler when I showed up in your shop? I know it's fake.'

Terrance shrugged. 'It's not fake. It's just empty. It's not even mine. A customer left it behind, but never came back for it. I kept it around just in case, but as you can probably tell, I'm not one for throwing stuff away.'

'But why pretend to need it?'

'I didn't want you to know it was me following you,

did I? That's why I acted like I didn't know you when you showed up at the shop waving some fake ID around. Those tour groups, they're all nutjobs and addicts. I get paid to run those classes, but I don't trust any of them. When I heard you heading up the path I wondered what you were up to, that's all. I do a bit of conservation work around the area. I've had them off setting fires, that kind of thing.'

'But why run off?'

Terrance gave an embarrassed smile. 'When you did that little army man roll, I got spooked. Thought you might pull out a gun.'

Slim nodded. 'I suppose that's understandable. I'm afraid I've never got over some of the things I saw back there in the desert.'

'Gulf War?'

'First. I was a kid.'

Terrance looked down. 'Better you than me.'

Slim walked over to the dresser and pointed at the family photographs. 'Who is he?' he said, pointing to the older man.

'Alan,' he said. 'And the older woman is Corrine, his mother. That picture was taken in 1968. I was eight years old.'

'And what is their relationship to you?' Slim asked, resisting the urge to grit his teeth, frustrated that Terrance was leaking him the information one piece at a time.

'They took me in off the streets.'

'They had street children in Totnes?'

'I was in care. Kept running away. Don't think it was

ever official, but they were good to me. Brought me up when no one else wanted me.'

'Who were your birth parents?'

Terrance shrugged. 'I don't remember them, have never met them, don't know who they are or were. They're likely dead; might as well be. What does it matter? They dumped me on the steps of an orphanage when I was a baby. It doesn't matter who they were.'

'Where did your name come from? Why "Winters"?'

'The orphanage named me after the season I arrived. I liked it better than "you damn boy". Alan wanted me to change it to McDonald, of course, but I'd got used to it.'

'That's not good enough.'

'What's not?'

'Stop feeding me a line. I've never heard of an orphanage assigning names like that. There was another reason they chose it, wasn't there? Tell me the truth.'

'Why do you care?'

'I have my reasons, and I have my suspicions, too.'

'Like what?'

'Take off your shoes. Show me your feet.'

Terrance stared for a moment, then burst out laughing. 'What?'

'I think you're a descendant of hers. One of her cursed. That's why you were abandoned, because old superstitions run deep in small towns. And that's why he took you in. And they named you "Winters" to mark you. Winter with an apostrophe. Isn't that right? Winter's descendant.'

Terrance shook his head. For a long time he stared at the floor, saying nothing. Finally, he said, 'Huh. You're good, I'll give you that.'

'Your toes are webbed, are they?'

Terrance shook his head again. 'They were, if "webbed" is what you want to call it. I prefer conjoined. Less fanciful. In any case, I had that crap fixed long ago, back in the eighties, as soon as I was old enough to sign the forms.' He rolled his eyes as he kicked off his right boot, then pulled off a thick fisherman's sock with one swift movement. He held up his foot and flexed his toes. Three moved freely, the other two as a single digit.

'The smallest two are fused,' Terrance said. 'I had the webbing removed from the others, but the last two couldn't be separated because the bones are connected.' He sighed, then pulled his sock back on. 'It's the same on both feet.'

'Do you know why?'

Terrance looked up at the ceiling. 'Genetics? Because some arsehole god hates me? I don't know. All I know is that the history of it in these parts got me labelled. School, until Alan had me moved and kept out of anything that required me to remove my shoes, was brutal. I was marked as some kind of sinner before I was old enough to know what one was.'

'And Alan helped you?'

'I was running away from care, running away from school. I met him down by the harbour. He took me in. He and his mother were good to me. Over time I became part of their family.'

'I've been trying to talk to him.'

Terrance shook his head. 'He's become reclusive over the years. Even I only see him once in a while, when he stops by for some tackle. And he sends me the originals of each one of his paintings, once or twice a month, like clockwork. So many I've had to start selling them.'

'What happened to him? Why won't he talk to me?'

'He doesn't like people. I moved out when I was eighteen. He was good to me, but he was never a real father. He had his ... reasons, for taking me in. I owe him respect, but there was never any love. Our relationship is formal these days, although I'll always be grateful for what he did for me.'

'And Corinne? Can I speak to her?'

Terrance's reaction, a scoff and a roll of the eyes, told Slim all he needed to know.

'She's dead, isn't she? He's claiming her benefits.'

Terrance pulled another cigarette from a packet and lit up.

'Look,' Slim said, 'I'm an alcoholic. I just broke into your house, and I'm wanted by the police for various other misdemeanours. Nearly twenty years ago I did some time because I tried to kill a man with a razor blade. Luckily for him and me, I was too drunk to pull it off.' He shrugged. 'It wasn't even the right man. It was someone else who was sleeping with my wife.'

'Why are you telling me this?'

'Because I have no moral high ground. I'm hunting a murderer. I don't care if someone's cheating the welfare state.'

'She's been dead for ten years or more. He had to tell someone, so he told me. I know he didn't kill her. He's just a recluse. He doesn't want the attention or the drama that would have gone with announcing her death. He sells enough paintings that he doesn't need the money. He only does it because he doesn't want people intruding on his life. For all I know he drops her pension into the charity boxes by the port.'

'And her body? Is she still in there?'

Terrance shrugged. 'I doubt it. Knowing him, he probably took her out on his boat and dropped her into the river. He's always been a fish out of water, has Alan. Never liked being on land.'

'I need to see him.'

'He won't see you. He has as little contact with people as possible. I arrange the printing of copies of his paintings, and their distribution. Makes up the difference in shop trade lost to the damn internet. That's one reason why he sends me the originals. I know he got cajoled into attending an exhibition a month or so back, and hated every minute of it.'

Slim smiled. 'I know. I was there. This is important, though. I need to talk to him.'

'He's not a bad person. Just … unique.'

'I'm not saying he is. I just need to clear him from my enquiries. If he's done nothing wrong, he has nothing to worry about.'

'Like I say—'

'I'm not planning to ask, Terrance. I broke into your fortress, didn't I? I can get into most places. I want you to take me up there.'

'When?'

'Right now.'

59

The sun was beginning to dip by the time Terrance's battered old car pulled up outside Corinne McDonald's house. Terrance started to get out, but Slim put a hand on his arm.

'Stay here,' he said. 'I'll do this alone. Don't even think about driving off or calling the police.' He patted his pocket. 'I have you covered.'

Terrance shook his head. 'He won't talk to you,' he said. 'He probably isn't even there.'

Slim climbed out, slammed the door, and made his way up the steps to the house. He glanced up and down the street, then reached forward and slid his pick into the lock. The door clicked open, swinging forward a few inches before a chain on the inside caught it.

'Alan?' Slim called into the gap. He waited a couple of minutes, but got no response. With a wry smile he reached into his coat pocket and pulled out a pair of pliers he had picked up in Terrance's yard and secreted away without the fisherman noticing. Pushing them into the gap, he twisted them around the chain and yanked hard. With a couple of further pulls the fittings ripped out of the door, allowing it to swing open. As he stepped inside, Slim glanced back down at Terrance, waiting in the car, wondering what the fisherman had seen, but Terrance was reading a newspaper he had brought with him. Satisfied, Slim stepped inside and pulled the door shut.

The house smelled of age, paint, and fish. The hallway was relatively cluttered, with several jackets hung on a rack behind the door, a couple of easels leaning against the wall, and even a box of fishing tackle sitting on an old-fashioned telephone table next to a dusty dial phone. Slim followed the cord back along the floor, lifting an eyebrow when he saw how it had been cut near the socket. Alan really didn't like intrusion into his life at all.

Slim opened the nearest door on the left. It led into a living room which was tidy and formal, perhaps because its window opened onto the street. Net curtains allowed light to enter, illuminating a faded and worn three-piece-suite and a couple of shelves of books, all local history or nautical-themed. There was no television, but a radio stood on a dressing table in the corner. The wallpaper was a dusty brown, a mantelpiece over an unused fireplace holding just a couple of generic ornaments which could have come from any local tourist shop. There were no family photographs or personal effects of any kind. No books left open on the arms of chairs, no newspapers or coffee cups, no pictures on the wall. The room felt like a museum display of 1970s England.

Slim closed the door and walked down the hall, past a set of stairs leading up. In a room straight ahead he found a small, cramped kitchen. The smell of fish pervaded from here, although there were no signs of anything having been recently cooked. No plates or cutlery left on the draining rack, and the sink's bowl was dry. In the cupboards Slim found cheap supermarket brand boxes of cereal, a couple of cartons of UHT milk, and a few tins of pasta sauce, all cheap, generic, simple flavours. It felt like a relief effort, and he wondered if Terrance shopped for his erstwhile foster parent.

A door at the back of the kitchen led into a small utility room. A couple of pairs of waders stood by a back door that opened onto Alan's garden. Outside was an overgrown yard with a few small shrubs forcing their haphazard way out of the surrounding brush. It looked like it had once been cared for, maintained, but perhaps this had been Corinne's domain, one left to literally go to seed since her death.

Slim went back through the house, into the living room, where he peered through a window to check on Terrance. The fisherman was still reading his newspaper.

On a landing upstairs, Slim found a vase standing on a small table filled with dusty dried flowers. Net curtains that needed a wash hung over a window that looked down onto the street. Slim glanced out once more at Terrance, still sitting in the car, then went to check the bedrooms. One was a guest room, all floral and lace. Dust plumed as Slim patted the pillows, and he retreated back onto the landing, a hand over his mouth to stop himself coughing. A bathroom at the end had another dry sink and a shrivelled bar of soap which hadn't seen use in several days.

The other bedroom, farthest from the street, was

clearly used. It smelled distinctly of paint, although Slim couldn't identify a source. The bedsheets were ruffled, partly folded back to reveal a sweat-stained sheet badly in need of a wash. A bedside table held a couple of books on local history, and a wardrobe in the corner, against the far wall, had a door that had got stuck on the corner of a protruding shirt sleeve. The wardrobe itself looked ancient, its knobs faded to a dull bronze, the chipped and scored wood dark brown, whatever design it had once held faded into the background. It had a small mirror in the door at head height, and the carpet in front of it was worn almost through, as though whoever used this room spent a lot of time perusing his appearance.

Slim went out, closed the door, and went back along the landing. Something wasn't right about the house, but he couldn't quite figure it out. For the residence of a man described as a recluse, there was very little about this house which suggested it. With a decent clean it could be rented out.

Slim was halfway down the stairs when he realised.

He stopped dead, staring at the wall across the hallway from the stairs, between the living room and the kitchen, at what should have been but wasn't.

The house was missing a room.

60

The light through the frosted window above the door revealed where the missing room should have been: a slight bulge in the wall where the doorway had been bricked up and wallpapered over.

Slim stared at it for a long time. The house was cramped enough as it was; you didn't hide a room without good reason.

Frowning, Slim studied the living room door, then looked back up at the landing. The living room wall on the hidden room's side was plain and unadorned, and the kitchen's fixtures were immovable. The house was part of a terrace, meaning it could have been offered for use by the adjacent occupants if someone had been prepared to knock through the wall, but that seemed unlikely.

Slim had seen no possible entrance. Heart racing, he ran back up the stairs and into the bedroom. He felt around the floor for a trapdoor of some kind, but found nothing. The bed was wire-framed, so Slim lay down and felt around underneath, pushing a few boxes of old fishing magazines aside, but again found nothing.

Finally, he turned to the wardrobe. The stiff door resisted his pull at first, but once open he found only a skeleton crew of clothing: a couple of shirts and an overcoat, arranged to hide the presence of a trapdoor in the floor below, a trapdoor with a handle caked with dried paint. It came up easily when pulled, revealing a dark space below, the light over Slim's shoulder illuminating the first few steps of a metal ladder leading down.

He had neglected to bring the torch hidden away in his belongings back in Eliza Turkin's abandoned house, but he had no choice. He might not get another chance to find out what Alan McDonald was hiding down there in the dark.

He climbed awkwardly into the space—clearly designed for a much smaller man—and started down.

Immediately, the smells that had pervaded the rest of the house blanketed his senses: paint, drying and wet, fish, both rotten and fresh, and something else: formaldehyde.

He stepped down onto the floor in the dim circle of light cast from above, and although the walls were hidden in gloom he realised he had found Alan McDonald's secret studio. The floor was bare stone, flecked and splashed with dried paint, and a multitude of easels stood around him like wooden statues, some containing half-finished paintings, others empty. Against the nearest wall was a ramshackle dresser scattered with painting equipment: brushes in filthy jars, scraps of canvas, dirty rags, small plastic bottles containing dozens of shades of paint.

As his eyes adjusted, the outline of something else appeared, something that dominated the room.

A bed.

And lying on the bed were two shadowy figures. Slim took a step backwards, a string hanging from the ceiling bouncing against his ear. As he lifted a hand and tugged the light cord, he saw one of the figures shift.

Light filled the room and Slim staggered, his resolve broken as a gasp escaped his mouth. He knew now where the stench of formaldehyde came from: not from the paintbrush cleaning fluid as he had assumed, but from the mummified corpse lying on one side of the bed, leathery lips pulled back over protruding teeth in a smile that Slim knew would haunt him for the rest of his days. Brittle hair hung down over bony shoulders, to a body covered with what appeared to be a dress woven from fishing net and shells.

Slim was aware of his knees hitting the floor. He stared at the corpse, barely aware of Alan McDonald sitting up, picking up a pair of spectacles from a bedside table and frowning through them at Slim like an old man woken by a noisy dog. Nor did he have more than a vague awareness of a shadow covering the trapdoor above, and a voice saying, 'Sorry, Dad, I didn't think he'd ever find it.'

Something heavy came crashing down, striking Slim on the side of the head. From the way it made a strangled ring he knew it was the old telephone from the hall, but it didn't really matter as he slumped forward to the ground, his vision blurring and then fading to black.

61

'What are we going to do with him?'

A sigh. 'What we did with the girl. We have no choice. Why did you bring him here? Why did you let him disturb her? *Why?*'

Slim became aware of the voices, but kept his eyes tightly shut. It wouldn't do for them to know he had regained consciousness. It was all he could do to suppress a groan or shift against the bonds tying his hands. His head was ringing, his hands and legs felt numb.

'He was persistent. I thought he had given up, but then he broke into my house and saw your paintings.'

'We have to protect her.'

'No. He doesn't know what he saw. Move her, clear out her things, hide her. They have nothing on you. On us.'

'You don't get it, do you? After all these years, I tried to drum it into you. It's them and us. They don't want our type, and they'll drive us out, like they drove her out, like they drove out Mistress Beatrice. We're not wanted.'

Terrance sighed. 'You can't just keep killing people.'

'Don't say that ugly word. I've killed no one.'

'Then what do you call it?'

'Look at her. Does she look dead to you?'

'Dad—'

'Enough. We need to get him out of here as soon as it gets dark. Out to the river. It can be done by morning.'

Slim heard a sniff. He frowned, unable to help himself. Someone was crying.

'Not again, Dad, please. Not again.'

Slim flinched as a heavy kick struck his stomach, knocking the wind out of him. He grunted and attempted to curl up, his eyes snapping open to see Alan McDonald standing over him, face in shadow.

'See?' the old man said, turning to Terrance, whose cheeks were wet with tears. 'You can't trust anyone. He was listening all the time.' He leaned down, face close to Slim, and Slim smelled fish on his breath, as though Alan McDonald ate them straight out of the water. 'Weren't you?' He turned back to Terrance. 'It's us versus them, I told you. We need to get rid of him.'

'Let me go,' Slim gasped.

Alan turned back and squatted down. The light caught his face, shadows filling the lines drawn by a lifetime in the sun, and he momentarily looked ancient, a relic of a man God had forgotten to claim.

'Like you would have let us go?' No longer was he the shy, nervous painter; on his turf Alan McDonald was king. 'You had every chance. I won't have anyone soiling her memory. I won't.'

'Is that what Carson did?' Slim asked, his breath slowly returning.

'Carson?'

'The radio DJ. The man who died.'

Alan flapped a hand and turned away. He walked over to a workbench and began tinkering with a series of glass bottles. Slim managed to twist enough to get a view of the other shape which had been on the bed, and it was as horrifying as he remembered before blacking out. At first he had thought it might be Alan's mother, Corinne, having remained here in death, but now he realised it was far too ancient for that. Bones had worn through the leathery hide in places, and Slim noticed how some patches of skin had been sewn back together, as though Alan was doing his best to maintain the corpse's condition even as it gradually fell apart.

'Where did you find her?' he asked. 'That's Eliza Turkin, isn't it?'

Alan paused, his hands going still. He didn't turn around, but Terrance rubbed a hand through his hair as though Slim had pushed one button too many.

'Just keep your mouth shut—'

'I didn't find her,' Alan said, interrupting Terrance. 'She found me. She called to me, her arm raised from the water. I had to answer. I had to protect her.' He turned around, his eyes narrowed. 'I promised.'

In his hand he brandished some kind of sponge pad. He crossed the room to Slim and held the rag over Slim's face. Slim struggled as a noxious smell invaded his senses. He knew what was happening, but bound as he was, there was nothing he could do to prevent it.

His strength faded quickly, his eyes closing.

∽

The Angler's Tale

When he awakened, he was lying in the bilges of Alan's boat, wooden slats pressing into his sides, the protruding heads of a couple of loose screws pressing into his back. A small engine was humming, and overhead, sea birds called as they swooped and dived. The smell of salty sea air did nothing to calm Slim's pounding skull, which felt as though someone had bashed it against a harbour wall. He tried to lift his head to look around, but gave up, lying back and listening to the sound of the river as they motored through the water.

'He's awake,' came Terrance's voice from the bow. Slim craned his neck and caught a glimpse of the fisherman sitting beside an outboard motor. 'Dad?'

'Good,' came another voice.

Slim tried to move his feet, but they were tied tight. The twine had slipped over his socks and now bit at his ankles. He recognised it as the same twine he had seen in the museum, binding stacks of prints. It made sense now; Alan, wanting to catch the sunrise, had been painting on the sandbar beneath the bridge when Carson had shown up with the prostitute.

'You left your string up there, didn't you?' Slim said, trying to force some strength into his voice, when all he wanted to do was throw up. 'You dropped it on the path before you climbed down with your painting gear. You'd moored your boat back along the bank in the trees, where no one would see it, and you'd carried your stuff down to the old bridge. The old man showed up with the prostitute, didn't he? He picked up your string and started making lewd suggestions. The woman ran off, and you closed in.'

Slim was still staring up at the sky as he spoke, but

suddenly his vision was filled with a shadowed view of Alan McDonald's face.

'You have so much to say,' the old painter said. 'He defiled my grandmother's resting place with those women.'

Slim took a few seconds to process the information. So Eliza Turkin was Alan McDonald's grandmother—the timeline made sense. But—

'Those women? More than one?'

'The older one ran off. I was actually thinking of climbing up and helping him when the younger one showed up. They did dirty things there, disgusting things.'

'Explain to me.'

'I'll not talk of it.' Alan growled with frustration, stalking up to the end of the boat, before returning again. 'When they were done, they argued. His feet were still tied. He slipped.'

'Did she push him?'

'Maybe. I don't know. I didn't see.'

'You could have called the police.'

'Why? The girl ran off. And have myself accused of his murder?'

Slim lay back in the boat. Eloise had somehow followed Kirsten and Max Carson, and had seen an opportunity to make herself known. It suited what Slim knew of Eloise's personality for her to have seduced her own father before making the big reveal. And then she had left him.

The outboard motor slowed. 'Bring it in slowly,' Alan told Terrance, as the boat began to turn. 'The bank is a little farther to the left. We need to put him in deep were he won't come bobbing back up in a few days.'

Slim tried to pull up his legs, but realised the twine around his ankles was tied to something else.

Bricks.

'Wait!' he said. 'We can talk about this. I'm not with the police. I don't need to say anything. I can made evidence disappear—'

Terrance laughed. 'So can we,' he said.

'It was people like you,' Alan said. 'Persecutors, conspirators, the lawmen. The ones who decided she wasn't good enough, that she was a freak. My grandmother never hurt anyone, but they made her suffer, as they'd made her mother suffer before her, as they made everyone associated with her suffer. Like they made the boy here suffer until I took him under my wing. You and your type have always been the enemy of ours.'

'I'm no one's enemy,' Slim said.

'You should have kept your nose out and stayed away. Just like that old bastard and his tarts should have stayed away. We don't want you here, but since you came ... we have a place for your type. Lift him, Terrance.'

Terrance pulled Slim up into a sitting position. He glanced around and realised the boat was floating just off the collapsed railway bridge. On the hill behind it, the empty windows of Eliza Turkin's old house watched him.

(watched him—)

She said she had known he was there, and had followed him. She said she had known his every movement. Was she watching him now?

As Alan twisted him around, tightening the bonds on

his wrists, Slim drew every last ounce of breath into his weakened, aching lungs.

'Marion!' he screamed with everything he could muster. 'Marion! *Mari*—'

Terrance's fist collided with the side of his face, knocking the breath out of him. It landed again before Slim could react, and he slumped sideways, crashing back down into the bilges of the boat.

'Hold him still—'

He felt something cold and hard rub along his wrist, the head of a screw worked loose over time from the boards it secured. Even though it was blunt, Slim hacked his wrists across it, not caring as it cut messily into his flesh. He needed only to loosen the twine a little.

'Hold him still, you idiot—'

Terrance grabbed Slim's wrists but blood from the wound had made them slick. His fingers slipped. He stepped forward, trying to regain his hold, making the boat rock. Slim leaned with the momentum and kicked out at Terrance, knocking him backwards. As Terrance stumbled back, making the boat rock even more, Slim jerked his wrists, feeling the bond fray further. Alan reached for him, but Slim lifted an elbow and jerked forward, trapping Alan's arm between his elbow and body. Alan jerked, but Slim held on, twisting with his other hand, feeling the twine dig deeper into his wrists. Terrance, trying to stand, caused the boat to rock even more. Alan screamed at him to stay still, but too late, Slim's right arm broke free, blood spattering across the bilges. He spun, clamped his arm around the old painter's knees, and rolled with the boat's momentum, knocking both Alan and himself over the side.

The shock of the cold had only just struck him when he remembered the bricks. In a moment he was plunging down, sinking fast, one arm still clamped around Alan McDonald's legs. The painter was kicking and struggling, but Slim held fast even as he felt muck thicken around his feet, aware that Alan would quickly run out of strength. As small fists pounded at his shoulders, he squeezed his eyes shut and hung on, concentrating only on holding his breath.

His senses began to darken. In his arms Alan fell still, and Slim felt certain he was no longer moving downwards. He began to dream of his childhood, of days left alone, of loveless birthdays, of his mother's rages over Christmas cards from his father, of the drink which had always numbed him. Feeling his own strength fading, he let go of Alan and spread his arms, letting the cold numb those parts of him the painter's body had kept warm, and he thought of days in the Iraqi sun and boots in the sand, of a razor blade, of a letter from an abortion clinic screwed up in the rubbish, of courtroom doors and the end of the world—

Hands closed over his shoulders and then he was moving. He opened his eyes and his mouth before he could help himself and water came bludgeoning in. He struggled even as someone struggled with him, but while his mind darkened his vision lightened and then he broke the surface, coughing and gasping for air as strong arms pulled him up on to a grassy sandbank.

'Hang in there,' came a voice from overhead, and Slim looked up, into the rising sun, and saw a woman's face silhouetted there, and in the absurdity of everything, he began to cough and laugh at the same time.

62

Involuntary manslaughter by way of self-defence.

He might have got off free, had it not been for a series of misdemeanours leading up to Alan McDonald's death which had soured Slim in the view of the court. Five years, two to be served behind bars, with three suspended. Plus, with good behaviour the judge said he might even be out in a matter of months.

It was the best he could have hoped for.

Marion had watched the proceedings, and met him outside as he was led away, allowed a few minutes with his counsel before beginning his sentence. In the weeks he had spent on bail while awaiting his trial, a lot of the pieces had fallen into place.

In addition to Alan's body, three others had been recovered after the inlet's mudbank was painstakingly dredged and searched. Two were ancient, dating back to the 1990s. One was a local man who had gone missing, another a tourist who had vanished without trace.

The third was Corinne McDonald.

The Angler's Tale

The remains of all three had been remarkably well preserved in the mud, making identification easy. DNA and dental records had been checked, but according to Marion, the corpses of all three had been nearly identifiable by sight alone.

A search of Alan McDonald's home had turned up a further two bodies. The mummified corpse Slim had seen lying on the bed was assumed, in the absence of any possible form of identification, to belong to Eliza Turkin. Later tests revealed traces of the same sediment found in the inlet by her old house, and assumptions were made that her corpse, weighted down in the silt, had come loose after the binding around her ankles rotted, and that the story Alan had told about Eliza hailing him from the water could actually be true.

Hidden beneath the bed was a final body. The skeletal, decomposing remains of a girl were identified partially by DNA analysis and partly by her half-sister, Lauren Trebuchet. She had died of strangulation, with particles of the same twine used to bind Max Carson's feet retrieved during forensic examination.

At his own trial, a tearful Terrance Winters admitted to kidnapping Eloise a couple of weeks after Max Carson's death on the orders of Alan McDonald, who had remembered her name from her heated final conversation with her estranged father. He claimed the kidnap to have been opportunistic rather than planned, after the girl unexpectedly visited his tackle shop one morning, wanting to purchase high density fishing line using a previously promised discount, the intended use of which was never determined. Later CCTV examination from street cameras across Totnes confirmed the girl's last movements, but in the absence of her body, she had never been investigated. Terrance also admitted to posting a letter found in the girl's clothing and addressed to Slim, hoping to deflect suspicion. DNA samples taken from skin oil residue on the letter Kim had saved proved a match. While taking the stand in court, Terrance begged the jury for mercy, claiming to have spent his life beneath his reclusive father's subtle power. The jury didn't agree, and he was sentenced to a minimum of fifteen years for aggravated kidnap and conspiracy to murder.

∽

For a long time, Irene Long's death remained a forgotten part of the puzzle. Just a week before his trial, Slim received a phone call from Kay.

'Hey, mate, how are you holding up?'

'Been better,' Slim said, trying not to think about his upcoming trial. 'Probably been worse too.'

'I mislaid something you sent me. So sorry it took so long to get back to you, but I thought you'd like to know.'

'Sure. Anything you have.'

'That list of medication you sent me … I had a contact run it against that autopsy report. You were bang on the money. Her medication was spiked. Irene Long, already dealing with psychosis issues, was inadvertently taking a combination of drugs which would cause heavy delusional periods. This girl Eloise likely poisoned her.'

Slim nodded. He thought about the death threats he had received, the likely attempt on his life. With most of the players dead, there were things he would never prove, but it appeared that both he and Irene had fallen foul of Eloise's delusional attempt to divert attention and suspicion from herself. Irene's bizarre suicide, brought on by the combination of drugs she was taking, and almost certainly Eloise's influence in a clumsy attempt to incriminate Slim, had drawn off police resources while retargeting the fingers of suspicion.

The girl must have thought herself a mastermind. Slim gave a wistful smile. He had read in a newspaper article that Eloise was now being posthumously investigated, both in the assault on the publican Jack Hodge and the suicide of her former boss, Leon Davids. Whether anything would come to it, he didn't know, but while he felt for Lauren, he would never forget how she had seemed when she told him of positively identifying her sister.

As though Eloise's death had been a relief.

∾

'You'll be out before you know it,' Marion said, pulling Slim into a hug as he stood waiting to be led away to begin his sentence. 'I know this hasn't worked out the way you hoped, but ... thanks. There'll be fallout for sure, but the last thing anyone needs to worry about is the damn tourist industry.'

Slim smiled. 'They'll be an extra stop on all those guided tours by this time next year.'

Marion laughed. 'I'll be staying away.'

'A good plan.'

Marion's smile faded. 'Your tipoff checked out, by the

way. I don't know if it would make any difference now, but I wanted you to know you were right.'

'About the car?'

'Like you said, it was the only viable way. Eloise followed Carson that first night on the tour, overheard their plans, and hid inside the car when they headed for Greenway. I had a mate from forensics search the boot, and we came up with hair samples which matched Eloise's DNA.'

Slim nodded. 'She hid under those nets in the back as they drove up there, then got out and followed them. After Kirsten ran off, Carson must have felt like he was dreaming when a young girl came wandering out of the woods.'

'At first.'

'Will any of this come back on Kirsten?'

Marion shook her head. 'I had the analysis done off the record. It wouldn't make any difference to your sentencing, and I think Kirsten was one of the few innocents in all this. For what it's worth, she told me she's thinking of changing profession.'

'She should consider starting an aquarium,' Slim said with a wistful smile. 'From the look of her place, she was halfway there already.'

Marion smiled. She patted Slim on the arm as though about to say goodbye, then her eyes suddenly widened.

'Oh, I almost forgot. I have something for you.'

'What is it?'

She put a hand into her pocket and pulled out a battered old Nokia. 'Yours, I believe?'

Slim couldn't help but laugh. 'Yes. What happened, did it ping off a telephone mast?'

Marion scoffed. 'You must be joking. This ancient thing was invented shortly after the wheel. It was found by a dog walker in a creek twenty feet back from the road. The guy handed it in to a local police station and someone must have had an old charger lying around. I guess you ... dropped it?'

Slim shrugged. 'Something like that.'

'It was traced back to you but didn't contain anything useable as evidence. I don't think it'll be missed.' She smiled as she turned it over in her hands. 'It still works, believe it or not.'

'Those things are indestructible,' Slim said.

'You can't take it with you so I'll have it sent to your home address.'

Slim smiled again. 'It will be nice to have an old friend waiting for me.'

Marion gave a sheepish smile in return. 'So, have you any idea how you'll spend your time on the inside? If you keep busy, it'll fly past.'

Slim nodded. 'I'm planning to take a rest,' he said.

END

ABOUT THE AUTHOR

Jack Benton is a pen name of Chris Ward, the critically aclaimed author of the dystopian *Tube Riders* series, the horror/science fiction *Tales of Crow* series, and the *Endinfinium* YA fantasy series, as well as numerous other well-received stand alone novels.

The Angler's Tale is the fifth volume in the Slim Hardy Mystery Series.

There will be more.

Chris would love to hear from you:

www.amillionmilesfromanywhere.net/tokyolost

chrisward@amillionmilesfromanywhere.net

ACKNOWLEDGMENTS

The Angler's Tale was something of a struggle. I picked Dartmouth for a location, and wanted the book to someone including mermaids. It did, in a sense ...

It's not always been possible for me to go on location for research, but on this occasion I could - spending an enjoyable day wandering around Dartmouth and visiting Greenway, which, believe it or not, I had no idea had once been owned by Agatha Christie. It added an interesting angle, however.

As always, I've taken massive liberties with my portrayal of location. Local residents will recognise some place and street names, and while some landmarks exist as described, others are entirely fictional.

Thanks this time to to my mother for undertaking a traumatic drive across Dartmoor to get us there, as well as to my regular contributors, Elizabeth for the cover, Nick for the proofreading, and the incomparable Jenny Avery for the fact checking and invaluable knowledge of pretty much everything. In addition, many thanks as always to my muses Jenny Twist and John Daulton, as well as to my wonderful Patreon supporters:

Alan McDonald
Janet Hodgson
Ken Gladwin
Rosemary Kenny
Sean Flanagan
Jane Ornelas
Gail Beth La Vine
Anja Peerdeman
Betty Martin
Katherine Crispin
Jenny Brown
Eda Ridgway
Sharon Kenneson
Leigh McEwan
Amaranth Dawe
Nancy
Ron

You guys are fantastic and your support means so much.
Happy reading,
JB

Printed in Great Britain
by Amazon